Atlanta

a novella

Loreen Niewenhuis

MAIN STREET RAG PUBLISHING COMPANY
CHARLOTTE, NORTH CAROLINA

Library of Congress Control Number: 2011923698

ISBN: 978-1-59948-291-0

Produced in the United States of America

Main Street Rag
PO Box 690100
Charlotte, NC 28227
www.MainStreetRag.com

To my sons, Ben and Lucas.
As always.

GRANT PARK — FIVE POINTS — GRANT PARK

I t is a velvet black night in Grant Park situated just south of Five Points, the core of the city of Atlanta. This neighborhood is slowly on the rise, swept along with the regentrification that trickles down from the neighborhoods north of Five Points and stabilized by the presence of the zoo. The Atlanta zoo is named — as if by a dyslexic — Zoo Atlanta.

The spring air is thick with humidity. Tiny tiger mosquitoes have to beat their wings extra hard to zip through the soupy air to swarm Bruce, the black man letting himself in to the junior high school. He wears the thick, dark blue cotton shirt and matching pants of a janitor.

His clothes are a couple of sizes too big, like he's planning on letting himself go. His slack face has three days' growth of stubble with many grey hairs — even though he's only thirty-five — that glitter in the halogen light. Bruce locks himself in the building and opens the janitor's closet. He pulls out the floor buffer, some large, round buffing pads, and a bottle of spray wax solution. He uncoils the cord and plugs it into the wall socket, centers the buffer over a pad and rests the handle against his thigh before taking rolling papers and a baggie of pot out of his pocket. Bruce rolls himself a joint. He licks it, twists the ends, and sticks it to his lower lip while he fumbles for his lighter.

H ours later, Bruce does the final buffing pass, a slow, side-to-side dance with the machine, waltzing it gently down the hallway with minute alterations in the height of the handle resting against the top of his thigh. The end of a glowing joint hangs between his slack lips. His eyes are half-closed. He notices something outside the narrow window in the door at the end of the hall. He releases the buffer and the machine slows and glides to a stop, thud-thudding against the base of the lockers. Bruce looks through the window dissected by the reinforcement wire imbedded in the glass.

Outside, Bruce sees a caped figure running around the playground, barely lit by the lights from the parking lot. The figure stops under the swing set and begins frantically digging with its hands. A plume of sand flings up in an arc. The figure takes out a bundle from underneath its cape and puts it in the hole, kicks sand over it and flies off into the night sky.

Bruce studies the vision, moving his sightline to various wired squares within the glass to see if the vision alters. He steps back and rubs his eyes.

"Damn," he says to himself. "Damn."

As the sun begins to bend its rays over the curve of the earth, Bruce leaves the school and shuffles to his battered, olive-colored sedan. During the night, pollen from the tall evergreen trees coated his car with a thin film so it looks a shade lighter than it actually is. He slides into the seat and slips the key into the ignition and turns it part way. He flicks the lever to scrape the pollen off the windshield with the wipers and fluid. He glances at the quiet playground, a look of panic washes over his face and he begins to hyperventilate. He starts the car and floors it out of the lot.

Bruce cruises the streets of Five Points, past the State Capital Building. The dome—which is actually gilded with gold from the mountains north of Atlanta—catches the clear morning light. He drives past without looking up at the glowing dome or even the blazing azaleas and flowering dogwood trees. His eyes dart side to side, searching for something else.

A few blocks away, he sees a young Latina woman in bright clothes, tall heels and fishnet stockings leaning on a lamppost near a bus stop. She's not there to catch a bus. He pulls over and she tap-tap-taps on the passenger side window with her acrylic nails and points to the seat. Bruce nods and she slides into the car.

"I'm Janine." She looks him over, noticing the baggy clothes. "You on Atkins or something, honey? Countin' carbs? 'Cause you dropping the L-B-S! Go up here and make a right."

Bruce follows her directions. His breathing is ragged and sweat rivulets run down his face despite the cool air pouring from the vents in the dash.

"Up two blocks, then left. I'll show ya." She points when they get to a narrow alley and Bruce makes the left.

"This here's my alley. Cops leave me alone here," she says. "All the way in, hon."

Bruce pulls up to the brick wall and stops. He turns off the engine and stares straight ahead at the brick wall, still clutching the steering wheel.

"Whatchu like, honey. I give you a price."

Bruce mumbles something and pulls a wadded bill out of his shirt pocket and lays his right fist on the seat between them.

"What?"

Bruce opens his hand to reveal a crumpled fifty-dollar bill.

"Ooo, baby, whatchu want me to do for this?" Janine takes the fifty and slips it into her cleavage like she's feeding a vending machine. Bruce stares straight ahead. "You got to tell me whatchu want, honey. I have many talents, but reading minds ain't among them."

"Just...hold my hand," Bruce whispers.

"What?"

"Please. Just hold my hand."

"That's all?"

Bruce finally looks at Janine. "Yes. Please. Ma'am."

Janine loses the hard look of the street, along with her accent. "Why would you want me to do that?"

"It calms me," Bruce whispers. "When I see things... things that aren't there...I need to get calm. Fifty for five minutes, then I'll drive you home safe."

There is tinny laughter from somewhere. Janine pulls out an earpiece. The laughter gets louder.

"Shut up, you dogs," Janine yells into her cleavage. She pulls the fifty out and stuffs it in Bruce's hand. She gets out and holds onto the car door as she teeters on her high heels. Janine addresses her cleavage again, "One of you guys get to dress next time. See how far you get in fishnets and—" She listens to the voices in her earpiece again. "No! I'm not going to bust this guy for paying me to hold his hand! Assholes!"

Janine leans into the sedan. Bruce fiercely grips the wheel, his head bowed in shame. His neck gleams with sweat.

"Hey," she says. Then, softer, "Hey."

Bruce turns to the sound of her voice.

"You seem like an okay guy. Go home. You got someone at home?"

Bruce shakes his head.

"Oh. Get a puppy. I hear it helps. Okay?"

Janine's ear piece erupts in laughter again and she tugs at the wire, pulling a microphone and tiny power pack out of her blouse. She turns it off.

"Take care backing out." Janine gently closes the sedan door and totters off.

Half an hour later, Bruce sits at Millie's Diner as he does every morning. It is a tiny dive filled with middle-aged and older men, mostly. The regulars.

Millie, a large woman stuffed into an industrial white waitress dress two sizes too small, shuffles along the counter pouring coffee refills. She's in her sixties and will probably die on her feet here one day. She will topple over and squish onto the floor, her feet with their worn, white shoes and baggy-nyloned ankles flopping upward from the force of her fall, then settling back down, prone and still. She's not a very good coffee pourer, or maybe she doesn't care if she spills. The regulars know enough to keep their hands away from their mugs as she shuffles past sloshing their cups with hot coffee.

"God hates ya'll. Every single one of ya," Millie drawls as she replaces the empty pot on the burner. The regulars don't attempt to argue.

She plates Bruce's eggs and slides them down the counter. "I know you like 'em scrambled, but my whisk broke." She addresses everyone in the room, "Ya'll hear that, you losers? No more scrambled till one of ya buys me a new whisk!"

The regulars grumble and debate whose turn it is to buy something for Millie.

After breakfast, Bruce parks in front of his shotgun house in Grant Park. Most of the other houses on his street have been freshly painted or sided, many now have additional rooms or larger porches attached. Several even look like someone dropped an enormous new house on top of the little one that was once there. Only Bruce's looks like it did forty years ago. The years have sagged the porch and left the clapboards almost entirely denuded of paint. There is an ancient dogwood out front and several overgrown azaleas, though, that obscure most of the demise with their brilliant floral display.

Bruce plods up the porch steps. He picks up the rolled newspaper and lets himself in with an old brass key worn bright with use. In the front room, Bruce has to turn sideways to make his way through the towering stacks of newspapers and magazines. Dust dances in the shafts of sunlight that make it through to the alleys between the stacks.

Bruce makes it to the sofa and sits. He tosses the

paper onto the coffee table strewn with rolled papers and magazines. A cluster of prescription bottles crowd one end. He opens them and removes one or two pills from each until his large, calloused hand is full of the multi-colored capsules and pills. He picks up an open can of Coke from the table and swirls it to see if any liquid is left. He lifts it to his mouth, drains it, shovels in the handful of pills and swallows them all with one terrific gulp.

Bruce reclines on the sofa and puts his feet up on the far end. With each place he compresses the couch, a puff of dust rises and dances above him in the shafts of light. Bruce watches the dancing dust, then raises his thick, weary arm and settles it over his eyes.

Janine walks up the six flights of wooden stairs holding her high heels. A sliver snags her fishnets and she clamps a hand over her mouth to muffle the obscenities.

Down the hallway, she slips her key into the door and unlocks it. There are two delivered boxes stacked up outside. She knocks lightly four times before opening the door. Her roommate, Paul, sits in the small room. He looks like he's been waiting for her to come home. He lights up when she enters.

"Tough night, dear?"

Janine shoots him a caustic look. She drops her heels and takes her gun from the back waistband of her skirt and places it on the small desk by the door. She pulls the boxes in from the hall and stacks them under the desk. After closing and locking the door, she flops into the chair near Paul and stretches her legs out to him. He massages her feet and a look of ecstasy washes over her face.

"You got a run in your new hose!" Paul says, turning her leg to see how far it's gone.

"Yeah. That sucks."

"I'll get you some more. I found some on eBay."

"Thanks. I always like to look my best when hookin'

for the department." Janine notices the circles underneath Paul's eyes. "How was your night?"

"Fine."

"The family?"

"They are...happy."

Janine moans as Paul works on her instep.

"Oh, that feels great, but I need to find my bed."

"What about your lunch?"

"I'm sleeping the rest of the—" She looks at Paul. "Is that today?"

"Afraid so."

"Can't you go to lunch? My mom loves you!"

In Paul's eyes are a thousand reasons why he could never go, the foremost being that he hasn't left this apartment for nearly two years. "She only likes the concept of me. Take a nap. I'll wake you. And I'll draw you a calming bath before you go to lunch."

"With?"

"Lavender for stress. Salts for fortitude. Ginger for truth."

"Then, can you hold me under the water for five minutes?" Paul smiles. "Ginger for truth?" she asks. Paul nods.

Janine shuffles to her room and closes the door behind her. Paul looks at her bedroom door with a level of contentment that says that he could stare at it all day. He's done it before.

That afternoon, long after Janine has left for lunch, a loud, double knock on the apartment door startles Paul.

"Erma's Market. Delivery," a man's voice says from the hall.

Paul stands. His eyes dart around the room. Another knock.

"Groceries. Hello?"

Paul goes to the small desk and opens a drawer. He pulls

out a pair of new, white cotton gloves and slips them on.

In the hall, Ken sets down the groceries and a six-pack of beer at his feet. He's a robust guy with shaggy hair in his late twenties. He wears a bicycle helmet and he's dressed in baggy shorts and a worn 'Erma's Market' t-shirt with a caricature of an old woman's face on it. He pulls the order form from his shorts pocket and consults his watch. "Hello? Groceries?"

The door snaps open and stops abruptly on the safety chain. Ken looks through the opening at Paul's wide eyes.

"Hey. I'm Ken. New grocery guy."

"Erma?" Paul gasps. "Erma!"

Ken points at the cartoon woman's face on his shirt and says, "Hip. Cracked. She's off deliveries for a long time, I'm afraid."

"I was...used to Erma."

"We're all used to Aunt Erma, my friend. Now we have to adjust to her ranting at us every day at the store instead of us waving at her wide backside as she rides off on her trike."

Paul blinks several times. "She rides a tricycle?"

"Yeah. Grown human-sized, red with dual baskets, front and rear. Actually has the two wheels up front and the single in the back. Radical." Ken stands taller. "It's my ride now. I'm going to airbrush flames on the fenders." Ken extends his right hand toward the opening in the door. "Hey. I'm Ken. Erma's nephew."

"Oh. Kenny," Paul pauses to catch his breath and steps back from the door. "I thought you were an artist."

"In the flesh! Delivery guy by day, artist at nights and weekends! Hey, open up. This is my last delivery, so I have time to crack one of these microbrews with you!" Ken looks from Paul's eyes down to his white gloves and retracts his hand. "Oh, hey, you're that Paul guy, right? Sorry." Ken thumps his head with the heel of his hand. "Shit. I thought you were a Monday delivery. Aunt Erma's going to kill me."

"She told you about me?"

"Dude, she merely made the rules very clear and told me to treat you right. I screwed up. I'm, like, really sorry." Ken pulls out the order form again. "It's twenty-two, fifty-three."

Paul slides two crisp twenties through the crack in the door. Ken takes them and starts rooting around in his pockets.

"No change," Paul gasps.

"Dude, I owe you, like, seventeen—"

"No change! Please!"

"Right. Germies. Sorry." Ken turns to leave.

"Ken. Wait." Paul points a gloved finger through the opening of the door. "Take... beers."

"What?"

"Take two beers. For the road."

Ken hesitates, then crouches by the beer. He pulls one out of the carton. "Thanks, I'll see—"

"You must—take two."

Ken shrugs, nods and takes a second. He stands and walks away. Over his shoulder he tosses: "I'll try to follow the rules better next time, dude."

Paul slumps against the door, closing it. His face is awash with sweat and his heart races, but a small smile plays briefly on his face. Paul loses track of time sitting there, but he eventually notices that he's still wearing his gloves. He takes them off and slides them back into the drawer. He clicks a button on a remote and opera music flows from speakers.

In his bedroom, Paul sits at his computer in the corner of his claustrophobic room. There is barely space for his small bed, desk and dresser. The window sill is jammed with flourishing houseplants, a shock of green in the otherwise off-off-white room.

Paul is only in his late twenties, but has the worry lines

of an old man. He turns his computer on and watches a cartoon world come into focus. On the screen, a cartoon family of four sits in a lavishly furnished living room. The family consists of two men and two children, a boy and a girl. Paul clicks on the children and moves them to their bedrooms. The kids twirl around and their clothing changes into pajamas. Paul clicks them into bed and says, "Good night, my darlings."

When Paul clicks on the men, they dance together. He moves the cursor over one of the men and Paul clicks the words 'Give a Hug.' The men hug and the contentment levels displayed above each man increases.

Paul leans back in his chair and watches the men embrace.

BUCKHEAD

The north side of Atlanta is where the money resides. There is so much money up here that enormous upscale shopping malls are built side-by-side. Or, in the case of Phipps Plaza and Lenox Square, diagonally across an intersection from each other. There are many guarded communities and some houses large enough to require their own personal remote-controlled gates. The money must be protected so it can be transported in BMWs, walked into the malls on Milano Blanics, carried in the coveted Hermes red Birkin handbags, then handed over for more costly things to be transported back behind the gates once again. If Atlanta had more natural water, many of these houses would add a moat and drawbridge to their ramparts. It would quickly become *de rigueur*.

In a trendy Buckhead restaurant, Janine sits across the table from her mother. Janine looks different with her hair and makeup calmed down. She eats a fancy, winged chocolate dessert like something imagined by the architect

Santiago Calatrava. Her mother has a cup of tea. Janine occasionally opens her mouth to say something, but her mother keeps talking, on a roll, a steamroller.

"...nice young man? There is a new gentleman at the condos! Miguel! Now he's divorced, but who isn't now-"

"Me," Janine interjects as she studies the support system of her cantilevered dessert.

"-adays? One kid, and I think he gets along with his ex, which is a plus-minus."

"What?"

"I'm never sure how to score that."

"Please don't fix me up ever again, Mother."

"Why? Is Paul going to make an honest woman out of you?"

"No one has to make—and Paul's my best friend, Mother, you know that."

"When will you be done playing policewoman?"

Janine glares at her Mother.

"How will you ever find a man if you're wearing that wretched gun on your hip?"

"Mother—"

"Men can be intimidated by a woman with a gun! Just because your father was a policeman doesn't mean you had to be one. And I couldn't take it if you—if you got hurt or—or gunned down like your father."

"I found someone, Mother."

Her Mother's face lights up. "Really? Who is he? Does he have a steady income? That is so important!"

"I work, Mother."

"Yes, but if you play your cards right, you won't have to." She fingers the expensive string of pearls around her nipped and tucked throat.

"Now tell me all about him! Are you in love?"

Janine leans across the table and—surprising even herself—nods.

HAPEVILLE

On the far south side of Atlanta is an area called Hapeville. Hapeville was a primarily black neighborhood when working class blacks wanted to live close to Five Points where they had mostly service jobs. When Atlanta started to build up about fifteen years ago, Latinos flooded the neighborhood. The new city was—and continues to be— built largely on their backs. Now their kids, true American kids, grow up in Hapeville and want more. Like all true, American kids.

Hapeville is the wedge that causes Highways 75 and 85 to split. The neighborhood rests atop the Hartford-Atlanta airport. Immediately beyond the airport is The Perimeter, Highway 285, sixteen lanes wide at its zenith as it encircles all of Atlanta like a roaring lasso.

Hapeville has a buzz to it, but it is not the buzz of a happening place like Buckhead. It is the buzz of a place demarcated by superhighways and a major airport. That inescapable buzz is machines, engines, tires grabbing at the road, planes screaming as they strike out into the sky.

Hapeville is not the cool part of Atlanta, which is north, a lifetime away. Well, not that far, actually, because Atlanta is one of the handful of American cities that has a working public transit train. The Marta system will, for a token's price, zip these true American kids to Buckhead, Morningside, Ansley Park, and even Decatur to see how the other half lives. Hapeville has its merits, though, as it provides a place for the independent business person to make a living since the big-box store scouts don't see enough money there. The scouts keep watching, though, as the housing prices creep upward. They hope that these people without money will be pushed further south, out of the city, so that the moneyed people can renovate their houses and shop at the new big-box stores they will build.

Until that happens, Chantel will run her little pet store next to the Margolis Beauty School. Chantel is in her early thirties, she is black and her hair is coiled into short, soft springs all over her head. She can look nothing short of optimistic with such happy hair.

She speaks into the phone. "Just tell Dr. Vlack that I'm worried about Bruce, that's all." She watches a glass repair guy pop out a piece of plywood from the front window and replace it with a new glass pane. "I'm aware of the clinic's policies, but if you look at my brother's chart, you'll see that I'm authorized to get updates even though my brother and I don't really talk." Chantel sighs and nods. "Please take my name down for Dr. Vlack. It's Chantel. 'C' as in 'Cathy'… 'Charlie'! 'Cocoa'!" Chantel presses her hand down on the top of her head, squashing her hair springs. "Sorry. 'Cathy' can be 'C' or 'K.' Dealing with this stuff makes me nervous." Chantel nods. "Yes. That's it. Same last name as Bruce. Thank you."

She hangs up and releases her hand from the top of her head to allow her hair to sproing back. She wanders to the front window as the repair guy puts the bead of sealant on it. He stands. "All set. Want me to get rid of the plywood for ya?"

"No," Chantel answers. "I'll keep it in back." Chantel signs the papers for the guy and he leaves. She looks down on the heap of sleeping Labrador puppies in the front window. There are eight: black, chocolate and yellow all from the same litter. The largest one is a yellow lab so light he's almost white.

Smiling, she wanders back to the baby bunny pen and dumps fresh wood shavings into their enclosure, smoothing them around with her hand. The bunnies hop around playfully. She gently lifts one and cuddles it against her face. The bell on the door rings and Chantel turns. Janine stands there. She holds a bouquet of flowers, pink and yellow roses mixed with spring daisies.

"What in the world do we have here?" Chantel asks the bunny.

Janine walks to Chantel and holds the flowers out to her. The bunny nibbles on one of the petals as the women lock eyes.

PIEDMONT PARK

Piedmont Park is nearly two hundred acres of green within this city that is building something on every open lot. Where there are no empty spaces small houses are knocked down for larger ones, medium office buildings crushed for high rises, whole apartment complexes obliterated for upscale condos. Parking lots are dug up for the foundations of mini-skyscrapers and parking is pushed underground, expanded, but downward, subterranean.

There is always room for more growth; one just has to be creative.

Atlanta is a city remaking itself as radically as after Sherman's march and burn. The only major tract of land to remain unchanged is expansive Piedmont Park that holds its ground between Virginia Highlands, Ansley Park, and Midtown. The residents of these neighborhoods often walk the park to forget their rising property taxes, the hellish commute, or their two-hundred-year-old oak tree that was vivisected and carted away to make room for the expansion to their house (that work-out room they've always wanted even though they never, really, seriously work out).

Even Piedmont Park isn't immune to multi-usage, though. Back in the mid-nineties, the east side of the park was scraped away and the tendrils of a water treatment facility were buried there. The park was re-seeded, new walking paths were installed, and everyone has forgotten what percolates beneath their feet.

Today in the park, the Atlanta Dogwood Festival is in full swing. The park is in riotous spring bloom mode, the dogwoods and azaleas coordinating to splash the green-green park with fuchsia and white and red. The ancient magnolias near the pond have even held their blooms for the festival, their creamy white, dinner-plate sized blossoms weigh heavy on the old branches; their sweet smell wafts on the breeze as the first of the petals let go and thud to the ground.

Artists' white tents sprinkle both sides of the paved walkways. Food vendors' vans congregate where the walkways cross. The smells of hot oil and spun sugar surround these intersections and drift to thinly coat the leaves and flowers of the trees with a slick, sweet residue.

Lorraine strolls along the path in the late afternoon, searching the artists' tents for something special, something to set off a space. A piece of art not for her home, but for a psychiatrist's office she has been hired to decorate. She wears a flower print dress of oversized red poppies on white. It flows in folds along her knees and her nyloned legs stretch down to her heels. Lorraine is a Southern woman in her forties. She is one of the few true Atlantans in a city full of people who have migrated here. One who is trained to dress properly and to never, ever sweat.

She stops at a tent filled with pieces of woven wire in copper and brass and steel in forms of abstract baskets. Lorraine is intrigued and touches the wires that extend from the edge of one of the baskets like antennae.

Ken sits behind the table in the tent, reading a book. He wears a baggy new 'Erma's Market' t-shirt and his hair is slicked back. He watches Lorraine examine the baskets, then says, "That one is stainless steel and brass. Some of the others have copper with the stainless."

Lorraine lifts one up and looks at the price. She sets it down again.

"The ones with copper aren't as expensive."

"Are you the artist?" Lorraine asks.

"Yes."

"Always sell a customer up."

"I think art should live with people. It's better than getting packed up in my aunt's basement till the next art festival."

"Y'all's price point is low for this quality."

"You're welcome to pay more."

Lorraine pulls out her card and hands it to Ken.

"LM Interior Design," he reads, "are you 'L' or 'M'?"

"Both. I'm Lorraine Miller."

Ken looks at the card again and smirks. "Right. I just had to read the next line and I would have figured that out. I swear."

Several people crowd into the small tent. One man hands a basket to Ken to wrap. When the transaction is done, Lorraine and Ken are again alone. "I want three of these," she says to Ken. "Are you able to deliver them to my home? I live over a few blocks on Drewry."

"Sure," Ken says as he stands.

Lorraine looks at his t-shirt and shakes her head. "What's with the t-shirt?"

"Oh," Ken looks down at the cartoon of his Aunt Erma on his shirt, "*quid pro quo* with my aunt." He points to her face. "She provides a workshop in her basement, I advertise for her at festivals."

"You may want to get a smaller size."

"Why?"

"Look around you. You've got all these rich women from Buckhead. And all the men from Midtown cruising the tents. And they're not just looking for art."

"I'm not—"

"No one said you were. You'd just give all of the ladies and gentlemen another reason to look at your...um... baskets."

"My art does fine, but thanks for the marketing advice."

Lorraine shakes her head. "You do give the standard twenty percent discount to designers, correct?"

Ken nods and moves around from the back of the table. "Which ones would you like?"

Lorraine points to three of the largest baskets in quick succession. Ken carefully stacks and takes them behind the table. Lorraine opens her purse and studies Ken again. "The standard designer discount is ten percent, Mr. Erma's Market. But how about you give the additional discount for cash payment?"

Ken isn't sure of her meaning.

"Sweet Jesus in heaven," she says. "You pay taxes on everything, don't you? Even what people pay in cash?"

Ken blushes. It is barely perceptible beneath his tan. "Yes ma'am, I do."

Lorraine chuckles, a tinkling, crystalline, horrible sound.

FIVE POINTS

Bruce sits in the sweltering waiting room in the social services building in the city center. He wears his work uniform even though he does not work tonight. He leans forward off the hard plastic back of the chair and rests his forearms on his thighs. His tremulous hands hang loose between his knees and he stares at some point in the air between his unstill hands and the worn linoleum floor.

An older black man sitting next to Bruce mutters to himself. Something about the relationship between AM radio waves and the texture of mashed sweet potatoes. Two skinny white guys stand near the door. One guy wears a NASCAR t-shirt with the sleeves cut off to reveal his tattoos. He's telling the other guy with greasy hair that he's here by court order because he pounded on his girlfriend again. And, by the way, she's pregnant. The greasy guy shakes the

NASCAR guy's hand to congratulate him. The NASCAR guy puts his thumbs in the waistband of his ratty jeans and says that this kid will make five. Finally enough for a basketball team.

"Bruce?" The nurse motions him back. "Sorry for the wait. Crush time out there." She trots ahead through the maze-like hallway and waves him into a tiny room with two chairs. Bruce assumes the position he held in the waiting room. "Might be a bit still," the nurse says as she closes the door and slips his thick file into the holder on the outside.

What sorts of things are you seeing?" the doctor asks Bruce when he gets into the room almost an hour later.

"Things that aren't there."

"Do they talk to you? Are you hearing voices?" Dr. Vlack wears an expensive suit and silk tie. He seems a little harried, but ten minutes in this place would have that effect on anyone. Dr. Vlack is in his early sixties, with salt and pepper hair and full beard gone completely grey.

"They don't talk."

"How do you differentiate between what's real and what's not?"

"The not-real stuff is…scary."

"Look at me, Bruce." Bruce tries, but his eyes drift away from the doctor's face. He looks at Bruce's shaking hands. He opens up the chart. "Who did you see last time?"

"Don't remember…some short woman."

"She increased your Klonopin?"

Bruce nods.

"There's a new drug that I'd like to try." He makes some notes in the chart. "We're going to stop the Klonopin and taper back your lithium a bit and add this new drug which you'll take only in the evening."

Bruce nods.

"Do you have someone dispense your meds for you?"

"Me."

The doctor writes out a script and clearly prints instructions on another piece of paper. He holds it out for Bruce. "Two lithium in the morning, one at night. Take the new pill with the evening lithium. Only take one. And only at night because it may make you drowsy. No more Klonopin. And stop taking the Wellbutrin, too. This new med should help you concentrate. So, how many pills a day will you take?"

Bruce studies the note, then looks at his unstill hands. "Two pills in the morning, two at night."

"Excellent. I want to see you back here next month, and call before that if things get worse."

"I'd…a puppy."

"Pardon?"

"I'd…like to get a puppy."

"How's your job going?" He flips the chart open, then shut again. "You work twelve hours a week, right?"

"On the weekend."

"Doing?"

"Floors."

"And how's that going?"

Bruce nods.

"And your home life? You live alone, right?"

Bruce nods again.

"Let's see how you're doing next month, okay? Remind me next time."

The doctor stands and patiently waits for Bruce to follow him out of the tiny room.

ANSLEY PARK

Hours later, Dr. Ira Vlack parks his Lexus in his carriage house garage. In the main house, his cats greet him, then run to the front door, which he opens. He steps out onto the porch and looks at the neighborhood. Even in the twilight, the azalea and dogwood blossoms are gorgeous. He moves to the plush front porch furniture and sits.

Ansley Park is a grand, old neighborhood, and Ira's house is one of the grandest on the curving, hilly street. It has a pillared, wrap-around, glorious Southern porch. Ansley Park is exclusive by virtue that you had to have a swimming pool full of money in order to buy into the historic neighborhood, and a cartload of cash to join Ansley Golf Club (complete with pool and tennis) that the neighborhood nestles to its bosom to protect it from non-members.

Ira's wife was old money from Macon. He is old money from Savannah, so they had purchased one of the largest homes in Ansley Park set up from the winding road on a hill, painted in period colors, a grand dame Victorian. Shortly after they moved in, they had the kitchen Wolf-ranged, Sub-Zeroed, and granited. When Ira's wife died two years ago, he couldn't think of moving from their home of over thirty years, couldn't do more than donate her clothes to charity so they could be of use to someone. Even that took him over a year to accomplish. Ira and the cats still feel her presence in the house, so they don't consider a move to a smaller, easier-to-manage place. The only change in Ira's schedule since Betsy's death is to volunteer one night a week at the free clinic downtown. His private practice is successful, so much so that he's having his office redecorated by LM Interior Design, but he finds that working with the rich and successful is not as fulfilling as when he is able to pull someone back from the brink of madness and isolation at the clinic. In his office, he sees disaffected trophy wives, self-sabotaging millionaires, and the under- or over-sexed of Atlanta's upper crust. Sure, there is always work to be done on the psyches of the rich, but sometimes Ira wants to shake them, to show them how lucky they have been in life. To tell them to stop, for pity's sake, stop whining!

Ira pats the seat next to him and the three cats jump up and crowd onto his lap. Ira strokes them as he looks out into the murky evening light. He watches a lawn crew finish up across the street. The three young, shirtless men toss their equipment into a battered pick-up truck. They speak in rapid Spanish to each other. Ira catches only a few words, and a name, 'Joseph.' When they look over at Ira's porch, he raises a hand to them. They stop for a moment, unsure how to respond, then continue loading their gear. Two of the men jump in the cab and the third hops into the open bed with the equipment. The truck, with its rusted muffler, roars out of the quiet neighborhood even though it is going slowly.

"Let's go see if we can find y'all some food," Ira says to the cats as he stands. They swirl around his legs as he shuffles through them and into the house.

HAPEVILLE

Margolis Beauty School sits on Old Jonesboro Road near the crossroad of Woodrow in Hapeville. The zip code is 30354. Zips convey status in Atlanta. Hapeville's holds no status at all. It brands you as poor, working class, probably Latino. There is usually trash on the burned up grass outside the Margolis Beauty School that is housed in a tired old Victorian next to Chantel's pet store. A drunk usually sits on the porch steps at night, tossing his empty tall boys onto the grass before falling asleep, curled on the welcome mat.

Giselle Margolis and her son, Manny, always pick up breakfast at the Mexicana Bakery between their small house and the beauty school. Manny is only four and Giselle cannot afford to have him in daycare with what she makes and what her ex-husband, Miguel, forgets to pay in child support. So, Manny has a corner in the beauty school filled with toys and a table with paper and crayons and a mat for him to curl up on when he gets tired. At the bakery, Giselle buys a black coffee, an orange juice, and three oreja pastries. She has them place the orejas into three separate, waxed bags. Manny always insists that they linger in front of the pet store window to see the puppies. Manny knows not to beg for a dog, but he cannot stop his heart from loving them, especially the fattest yellow lab. This dog is so pale in color his fur is almost white.

Upstairs from the pet store is the apartment where Chantel lives. It is a small place, basically one big room with a kitchen on one side and bed on the other. The most defining feature of the space is that the far wall is floor-to-ceiling shelves jammed with books.

This morning Chantel wakes, but not alone. Janine is still there, in her bed, her naked body partially draped with the sheet. Most of the flowers are in a vase, but some have been stripped of their petals. Some of these petals stick to Janine's bare shoulders, her back, her legs. Chantel raises herself on one elbow and kisses Janine's shoulder.

Janine inhales deeply and turns toward Chantel. Her smile could illuminate the room. It actually does. Chantel is bathed in the light of it.

When Giselle and Manny get to the beauty school, Giselle gently wakes the drunk on the welcome mat and sends him on his way with the extra pastry. Giselle drinks half of the strong coffee with her oreja and Manny eats his with his juice on the front porch. She and Manny sit together while she reviews the beauty school lesson for the day. Later, she situates Manny in his corner inside, a small alcove off from the main classroom where she can keep an eye on him. Then she drops a few ice cubes into her coffee cup and saves it for lunch.

The beauty school girls arrive at nine-thirty. School is supposed to start at nine, but no matter what Giselle does, how she threatens, she cannot get them there on time. It would do no good to fail an entire class over thirty minutes a day, so Giselle merely shortens their lunch break until it pretty much works out.

There are seven girls in this year's class. Lola and Rita are the most serious and come every day. Jennifer, Mary, Margaret, Thomasina and Lucy are a little more spotty in their attendance and attentions. Giselle is pretty sure she'll have to fail Lucy to protect the public from her lack of attention to detail. Like when to neutralize a perm she's giving to one of the other girls. Thomasina's buzz cut has grown out a bit and is cute on her, but when her scalp was all red and chemically burned, she looked like the lucky survivor of a horrible fire.

L ola and Rita always sit at the back of the classroom. Rita takes notes on the proper application of nighttime eyes while Lola doodles her boyfriend's name, *Joseph-Joseph-Joseph*, over and over in her notebook.

"Whatssat on your hand, Lola?" Rita whispers as she studies the bruised-looking back of Lola's hand.

"Bar scars," Lola answers.

"Oh, Jesus. Thought you got your hand caught in a car door or somethin'."

"Naw, they jez all have to stamp you so they know you paid. I got truly belligerent Friday night after about four tequila shots and a wet nipple."

"Where you bar hoppin' with your lawn jockey?"

"Lawn jockey?"

"Yeah. Joseph. He does lawns, don't he?"

"He a yard *MAN*. In Ansley *PARK*. Not a lawn jockey."

"What the diff?"

"I do believe that 'lawn jockey' has anti-racial tones to it. Anyways, Joseph and me jumped the Marta to Buckhead to party with the money. These clubs down here? They all trash once you been up in Buckhead. They got all that neon and John Mayer music."

"He's so cute."

"Really, you think so?" Lola asks.

"Yeah. Don't chu?"

"His mouth's too big. Looks like he could fit his drummer's cymbal in his big mouth, like, you know, you do with a piece of orange to make a goofy, orange grin?"

"I never noticed. Thanks, now you completely ruined my main fantasy. Now I have to go back to Mark Anthony or someone," Rita smirks.

"Told you he was a munchkin."

"That-did-not-stop-me, Lola."

"And he with J-Lo now."

"That-did-not-stop-me-neither."

"Well, then there's just no stoppin' you from fantasizing about a married munchkin."

"Least he speaks the spanglish."

"Oh, yeah, and there's such a shortage of spanglish-speaking munchkins around here. Why don't you go into the lettuce fields around pickin' time? You'll be up to your super-curled bangs in munchkin Mexicans."

"I ain't datin' no migratory types."

"That's the beauty of them, Rita, they fly away when you're done with 'em."

"You think I'm studying here soz I can get a migratory type?"

"Oh, yeah. We gonna end up in Buckhead after we graduate. They always lookin' for graduates of Margolis Beauty School up in Buck-Head."

"Teach used to do hair up there."

"Really? Why she back here with us?"

"'Bout the time she got divorced, her mami died and left her that tiny house she live in and this school."

"Maybe she can get us jobs up there!"

"Shh. She eyeballin' us."

Giselle pauses to do just that. She concludes her lecture with, "Remember, girls, there are no ugly women, only lazy ones. It is your job to use the full extent of your training to whip the lazy ones into shape." Manny knows that this line means the lesson is over for the day. He gets up from his napping mat and stands, waiting for his mom to pack her things.

Lola gathers her purse and notebook and smirks at Rita, "Teach ain't never seen my Aunt Rosa. She lazy AND ugly! Ain't no cure for that!"

VIRGINIA-HIGHLANDS — GRANT PARK — VIRGINIA-HIGHLANDS

Virginia Highlands, or The Highlands as the locals call it, is one of the coolest neighborhoods in Atlanta. It abuts Morningside — also very nice — and Midtown, and nestles against the east side of Piedmont Park. What sets Virginia Highlands apart is the delightful mix of commerce that runs through the middle of the neighborhood. There are trendy boutiques and restaurants, coffee houses, chocolatiers and bakeries. There is even a DVD rental place that is organized by the name of the director, not title. ('Because that's the way it's *supposed* to be arranged.') Streaming off the back of these establishments are medium-sized houses with mature trees in the yards, and squares of lawn possibly harboring militant fire ants. It is the rare neighborhood where you can actually take a walk *to* somewhere, maybe even run an errand on foot instead of constantly jumping in the car.

The neighbors all have their favorite coffee house where they know the workers by name. When they walk in the door, the barista asks, "Your usual?" and the person who lives in the neighborhood only has to nod, or, maybe, to feel more connected to this place that they imagine could not exist without their input into its perfection, might say to the multiply-pierced barista, "Please, Monikue," (carefully pronouncing the soft 'k'), "and how are you today?"

In the partially excavated basement of one of the medium-sized houses in The Highlands, there is a bare light bulb hanging in the dank, musty space. It doesn't throw much light because it is caked with dust. There is an old bathroom down here, the maid's bathroom from a time when the maids were black and had to use facilities separate from those the white families used. There is a pile of burlap bags next to baskets of old apples and sprouted potatoes. Tendrils from the potatoes reach out crazily like they're not sure which direction the light will come.

A pile of rags sits on the packed dirt floor. The rags move. It is a child. His name is Stevie and he is four. Or maybe five. Stevie can't remember if five comes after four and he's not sure when his birthday is. He is balled up for warmth...or maybe in fear. He mumbles to himself, "It's okay. I'll 'tect you." He talks to his fist in which he carefully holds a brown baby mouse. He raises his face and there is horror in his eyes: the whites of his eyes are blood red. His tears have partially washed tracks through the dirt on his cheeks. "I'll 'tect you," he tells the mouse again. He pulls a leaf from the potato tendril and feeds it to his mouse. Stevie paws through the rotten apples and pulls one out of the basket. He takes a small bite and places the piece on his hand. The mouse sniffs it and begins to eat. Stevie watches it and his mouth attempts to twitch into a smile. Stevie takes another bite of the apple for himself, careful to avoid the brown spots.

Footsteps click overhead and Stevie cowers and pulls the mouse close to his little chest. A sliding lock is thrown on the plank door and a shaft of bright light cascades down the wooden stairs as it opens, blinding Stevie. He squints and sees the legs of a middle-aged woman in expensive high heels and her full, flowered dress. She sets a paper plate and cup on the top stair, then closes and locks the door. Stevie never sees Lorraine's face. Her heels click away from the door and out of the house. Stevie's eyes follow the sound. He gently nestles the mouse in a nest of rags inside the potato basket. He waits until he hears the lock click on the front door and a car engine start before he crawls up the stairs and devours the food on the plate like a starving dog.

Next, he laps at the liquid in the cup.

Millie's Diner is empty now except for Millie. The lunch rush is over and she cleans up before closing for the day. A plate on the counter has a triangle of burger left on it. Millie picks up a knife to trim off the bitten part, then decides against it. She shoves the entire thing into her mouth.

The bell on the door rings, and Millie yells, "We're closed" but turns and sees Lorraine standing at the counter expectantly, her hands on her full hips.

Millie sneers at her, then scoops all of the loose bills and change out of her apron pocket and slams it down on the counter. She stomps off to the kitchen. Lorraine—Millie's daughter if one is observant enough to notice their matching noses—expertly straightens the bills. Then she sorts and stacks the change—fast, like a croupier—like she does this all the time.

Lorraine clicks into her neighborhood bank on her heels. She struggles to carry a small, heavy, canvas bag in one hand, her designer purse in the other. She swings the bag onto the counter where it lands with a thud.

"Hello, Lorraine," the teller says.

Lorraine nods and pulls out a roll of small bills and fans them twice before handing them to the teller. Next, she dumps out all the coins she has packed into paper sleeves. As the teller counts the bills, Lorraine pulls out a check from the Department of Social Services and endorses the back.

"And how is your young charge? I never see him around the neighborhood."

"I am home schooling him. He is a prodigy, I tell you!"

"Home schooling on top of your interior design work? My, my. And a prodigy? Well good for you. My youngest is barely passing sixth grade!"

"Bad apples are everywhere. I got me a good one this time. The younger the better, I say." Lorraine smiles a saccharine smile as she slides the endorsed check across the smooth surface.

GRANT PARK

Paul and Janine's small apartment overflows with an aria from Madam Butterfly. It is 'Un be di, Vedremo,' sung in Italian. This is the aria where she awaits the return of her lover, a song overflowing with hope.

Paul stands in the middle of the room facing the sound system. He wears only boxer shorts. His ribs, his vertebra are exposed as he lifts and lowers his arms. He is a strange bird soaring on the music.

"Tutto questo avverra, te lo prometto," the soprano sings. *"Tineti la tua paura—Io consicura fede lo aspetto."* The last sung note crashes and the music rolls over him, calms and fades.

Silence fills the room and Paul's arms fall to his side. He bows and takes several deep breaths as he returns to his body.

There is a soft knock on the door...four crisp knocks. Paul knocks on the inside of the door two times. A pair of soft knocks answers from the outside. Paul opens the door on the chain.

"Groceries," Ken says, grinning. "I threw in some extra stuff to pay you back the change. Oh, and an extra beer to make it come to an even twenty bucks this time."

"Please remove the extra beer," Paul whispers.

"Dude?"

"Odd numbers. Can't have odd numbers," he gasps.

"Right. Damn. Sorry."

Paul opens the drawer and puts on the gloves and slides a new twenty dollar bill through the opening. Ken gently takes it and pulls the extra beer out of the bag.

"I love Puccini," Ken says.

"What?"

"Madam Butterfly. Bitchin' opera. Saw it in Italy when I went over there in college." Paul presses nearer the opening in the door. "All that hope she has?" Ken shakes his head. "'Hold back your fears...*Io consicura fede lo aspetto*...I with secure faith wait for him.' Breaks your heart, dude."

Paul's mouth hangs open.

"K. See you next week." Ken walks toward the stairs. "Thanks again for the brew. No odd numbers next time!"

Paul watches Ken descend the stairs through the opening in the door, then closes the door and fingers the safety chain for a moment before removing his gloves and replacing them in the drawer.

HAPEVILLE

There is laughter in Chantel's bedroom and shuffling around on the bed. Janine and Chantel play with two of the Labrador puppies. The women wear t-shirts and boxer shorts. The puppies romp around attacking their hands, then rolling around with each other. The women upend the puppies and scratch their big puppy bellies.

Lovely.

Lovely.

Janine lies down and gazes at Chantel.

"What?"

"Just looking at you."

Chantel smiles. "We should hang at your place sometime."

"Um, yeah, sure."

"Are you worried about your roommate? We can do it sometime when he's not there," Chantel offers.

Janine chuckles.

"What? Is he a real homebody or something?"

"Yeah, you could say that." Janine pets the exhausted puppies. The two puppies snuggle together and fall asleep. Janine rolls onto her back and looks at the wall of books. She strokes the spines of a row of books. "Are they all fiction? No, like, 'How-to' or 'Self-Help'?"

Chantel goes with the change of subject. "Mostly fiction. There might be a couple books on how to build bookshelves. Ironically."

Janine looks at the wall of shelves. "You built this?"

"Yep. Trying to live up to the sterotype." She cracks herself up with this, but Janine looks blank. "You know, lesbian-boot-wearing-carpenter-house-builder?   You've never heard that?"

"Guess I wasn't delving into the stereotypes. Which other ones are out there?"

"Well, I'd probably be a 'lipstick lesbian,' you know, like Ellen." Then, off Janine's blank look, "Oh my god. Ellen Degeneres?? Like, the most famous lesbian EVER? Well, after Gertrude Stein. No, even more famous than her." Chantel looks for some recognition in Janine's face, but there is none. "Gertrude Stein? Writer? Hung out with Picasso?"

"Now, him I know. And that Ellen chick loves her dogs, right?"

"Sounds like you need a crash course in gay history, my love."

Janine looks conflicted on many levels by this statement. "Can't it just be me and you? Can we leave all the other gay women and my agoraphobic roommate out of this?"

"Seriously?"

"Yeah, like I don't want a history lesson. I'm not going to be marching in any gay pride parade."

"No, your roommate. He's agoraphobic?"

"Yeah, like severely."

"Meaning?"

"Hasn't-left-the-apartment-in-two-years severe. Only-talks-to-me severe." Janine looks at some books on the lower shelves and pulls one out. "Hey, here's one that's not fiction."

"That's about bi-polar disorder."

"Oh, hey." Janine looks at the cover of the book. "Do you have that?"

"No. My brother does. Bruce does."

"Oh. You said you didn't see him much. I didn't think…" Janine tries to joke her way around the topic. "So, maybe we should have all four of us together. Compare crazy notes and meds!"

"That's a little harsh, isn't it?"

"Sorry. My roommate and I keep it out in the open. And we do that through dark humor." Janine takes Chantel's hand. "Seriously. I'm sorry about your brother."

"Bruce."

"Your brother, Bruce." Janine realizes that they both have opened up here, so she takes another step forward. "I want you to come over. Meet my roommate. Meet Paul."

"Paul. I'd like that. You think he'll be okay to meet me?"

"I think so. He's heard me talk about you so much. He probably feels like he knows you already." Janine looks at Chantel. "He knew I loved you even before I did."

Chantel leans over and kisses Janine. "Just tell me when."

"How about tomorrow night? After we get back from Stone Mountain?"

Later that day, Giselle enters the pet store.

"Hey Chantel," she says.

"Giselle. Hi. Where's Manny?"

"With his dad. It's his weekend, and Miguel finally freed up his schedule enough to spend time with his son."

"Sorry. How's Manny taking everything?"

Giselle walks over to the puppy pen and pulls a sleeping puppy off of the top of the heap. She holds it up to her face and nuzzles the side of the puppy's muzzle. The puppy yawns and sticks out his pink tongue. "I don't know. He's not talking much these days."

"He never was that chatty, was he?"

"No. But now I have to pull everything out of him. And he still mostly responds with motions, you know? Nods and shakes. Talks with his eyes a lot." Giselle replaces the still sleeping puppy back on the heap and pets the velvet ears of several in the pile. "He loves these guys."

"Yeah. He's in here so much I think the puppies know him now."

"Do you know if he likes one more than the rest?"

"The biggest one. He calls him 'Whitey.' I heard him whispering to him the day you left him here for a bit while you went outside to chat with Lucy."

Giselle shakes her head, "What am I going to do with Lucy," she says, mostly to herself. "Wait, Manny was talking to the puppy?"

"More like whispering. I was cleaning the pen, or I wouldn't have heard him. He was having a whole conversation with Whitey."

"How big do these get?"

"They're labs, so seventy pounds for the females, eighty or so for the males."

"And Whitey?"

"Male. And from the size of his feet, he's going to be a big one, maybe pushing one hundred pounds."

"Do you think it will be strange for a Latina to be yelling 'Whitey! Whitey!' out her back door to call to the dog?"

Chantel laughs. "I think that will be a hoot, girl."

STONE MOUNTAIN

Janine and Chantel drive east on Stone Mountain Parkway. Janine drives but keeps glancing over at Chantel who stares out the window.

"Can't believe I've lived in Atlanta most of my life, but never made it out to Stone Mountain," Chantel says.

"Yeah, why is that?"

"I think my parents wanted to keep us from the carving on the face of it."

"So, you've never seen the laser show at night?"

"Laser show?"

"Yeah, they animate the carving, make the horses' legs move. It's like they're galloping along. It's pretty cool."

"Sure, if you're into that whole 'The South Will Rise Again' thing. That's not real big in the black community."

"I bet. Sorry. I never really thought about it, I guess. I like coming out to hike. Paul and I used to race to the top when we were kids. It was just a fun place to goof around."

"The Klan used to meet out here."

"Seriously?"

Chantel doesn't answer, just looks out the window at the large swell of granite in the distance. This is Stone Mountain, aptly named because it is a huge piece of granite that looks like an enormous sounding whale. This formation wasn't pushed up from under the ground as many mountains were, but rather formed underneath the surface and exposed by eons of erosion. It was there all the time, under the surface, waiting. It now looms seven hundred feet above the surrounding piedmont. Since the granite resembles a wedge, it is easy to hike the backside to the top, a gentle grade of rather flat granite studded with plants and trees wherever they can find the slightest fracture in the rock where a few grains of dirt accumulate.

Chantel's head swivels as the carving on the mountain comes into view. Robert E. Lee, Stonewall Jackson, and

Jefferson Davis all astride their horses, forever riding off to victory... somewhere.

"Hey," Janine says, taking her hand, "we don't have to be here at all, okay? We'll go somewhere else."

"No. It's fine. I'm making too much of it."

"Are you sure?"

"Yeah. Just no laser show, okay?"

About halfway up the mountain, Janine points to a bench and they sit. Birds flutter in and out of the thin trees on the mountain. Janine watches one land on a branch nearby, then she looks at a lower branch and sees a walking stick beetle. "Chantel," she says as she points it out to her. Chantel doesn't see it until it moves one of its legs. She jumps.

"It's a walking stick."

Chantel looks at Janine. "Now you're threatening me with nature?" They laugh together, and Chantel leans in for a kiss. Janine wraps her in a hug instead, glancing nervously at people walking by.

"It's like that?" Chantel asks.

Janine looks Chantel in the eye and says, "No. No, it's not like that, baby." Janine gives Chantel the kiss of her life, a kiss she feels in the core of her body, a kiss to lose herself in, to surrender to.

Chantel surrenders unconditionally.

As the women reach the top of Stone Mountain, they are holding hands. Chantel is out of breath, but Janine has hardly broken a sweat. "We're going to have to whip you into shape, baby," Janine teases her.

"I own a pet store," Chantel gasps. " I don't need to run down any bad guys." Chantel drapes herself over the railing on the top of the mountain that keeps people from launching themselves off the sheer face. She takes a moment to catch her breath. Janine rubs Chantel's back, then loops her arm around her lover's waist.

VIRGINIA-HIGHLANDS

The baby brown mouse sleeps swaddled in a rag in the basement. Stevie is not down here.

Lorraine sits at the kitchen desk at a computer. She hastily takes a simple alphabet test online, matching letters to images that begin with their sounds. Next, she matches up blocks of colors, careful to make an occasional mistake.

Upstairs, the bathroom is dark. Silent. Stevie sits shivering in a cooling bath.

"Get dressed! The social worker will be here in ten minutes," Lorraine yells up the stairs. Stevie stands and shivers even more as the cool, grey water drips off his body.

"Make sure you get all the dirt out of your ears this time!" she yells again from downstairs. "And I'm coming up in a minute to do the eye drops, so hurry up!"

Stevie wipes his ears with a white washcloth and looks at the brown spot. He swishes it around in the tub, and wipes his ears again. Satisfied, he takes a raggedy towel and wraps it around his shoulders as he steps out of the tub. He looks at the clean clothes set out for him. He holds up the underpants and stares at them like he hasn't a clue what to do with them.

Downstairs, later, Stevie sits crushed into the side of Lorraine on the big couch as she speaks to a woman in the big room. Stevie doesn't understand what they are talking about, so he concentrates on remembering how soft the couch is and how nice the room smells. He is exhausted and would like to fall asleep right here in this clean place, but he knows that the woman will get angry if he does. She may even decide to not feed him for a day or two again. Then there would be only the bruised apples to eat.

Lorraine suddenly pinches Stevie's side and he sits up tall. He must have missed something. The lady across the room is staring at him, waiting.

"Why don't you ask him the question again, ma'am. He was distracted when you first asked him how he likes living here."

"Stevie. Do you like living with Miss Lorraine?"

Stevie nods, big sweeping movements of his head, like he has been coached or coerced.

"And do you like learning on the computer?"

Stevie nods, even though he doesn't know what a computer is. When Lorraine pinches him again, he says, "Yes 'em."

"Well, Lorraine, I'll have a quick look at his room, then I'll be on my way."

Stevie watches in fear and amazement as Lorraine leads the short woman up the stairs instead of to the basement. He creeps silently behind. At the top of the stairs, Lorraine throws open a door to a bedroom filled with light and toys. The short woman opens up the dresser drawers and looks at Lorraine.

"Most of his clothes are in the laundry. I haven't had the time to do them what with the home schooling and all."

Stevie wanders into the room and Lorraine gasps. He walks the perimeter, touching things lightly to make sure they are really there.

"Do you like your room, Stevie?" the short lady asks.

"Yes 'em!" Stevie smiles at her. It is an unpracticed smile with the edges of his mouth unsure how far they should rise. Stevie places his hand on the bed and looks up at the hate on Lorraine's face. He retracts his hand, bows his head and goes downstairs to sit on the soft couch while he can.

Lorraine chats with the short lady while gently ushering her out of the house. After she's gone, Lorraine turns to Stevie and points to the basement door. Stevie begins to move, but Lorraine stops him with one word: "Clothes!"

Stevie strips and folds his clothes, leaving them neatly on the couch along with his shoes and socks. Soon, he wears only the new underpants, but the fly is in back. He descends the stairs as the door closes and locks behind him.

GRANT PARK

It is Saturday evening in Grant Park. Bruce waltzes with the buffer in the school hallway. His eyes are clear this time. He's not smoking pot.

Two blocks away, Paul and Janine set the table for three for dinner. Paul's hand shakes as he lights the candles and Janine notices. "You said you'd be okay."

"I am. Stir the sauce."

Janine stirs the sauce and Paul blows out the match and runs it under water before throwing it into the trash.

"Do you want your gloves?"

"You told her to not touch me, right?"

"Yes."

"Then I'll try it without the gloves. So it doesn't seem like such a freak festival."

"Paul…"

"Listen. You love her. I'm happy for you, and I want to meet her."

"And her brother…"

"Yeah. So, maybe she won't be freaked out by the freak fest."

Janine puts her arm gently around Paul and he tilts his head until it's on Janine's shoulder. "Stir the sauce. 'Constantly stir' is what the recipe says."

Janine releases him. "Taskmaster."

Paul pulls away and makes the sound of a cracking whip and they laugh together. The laughter of best friends that stops when they hear four soft knocks on the door. Paul stiffens and looks at Janine. "It's okay. I'll get it." Paul walks to the door and knocks twice. He listens to the responding knocks, takes a deep breath, and slides the chain out of the track. He holds his breath as he turns the knob and pulls the door open.

Chantel stands there with two bottles of wine, one red, one white. "Hi," she says, smiling brilliantly. "You must be

Paul. Welcome!" She looks panicked. "I mean, nice to…God, are you as nervous as I am?"

Paul exhales and laughs with Chantel. He steps back and motions her toward the kitchen and Janine.

Later, with dinner almost done and both bottles of wine nearly empty, the three of them chat away like old friends.

"Can I pour you some more red, Paul?" Chantel asks, placing a friendly hand on his arm. Janine's eyes go wide, but Paul nods and holds his glass toward her. She drains the bottle into his glass.

"Hey," Janine says, pointing at what just happened. "Hey."

"Oh, yeah," Paul says. "Cool."

"What?" Chantel asks.

"You touched me," Paul says, then he and Chantel break into song together, "And suddenly….Nothing….. Was…..the SAMEEEEEEEE!"

Chantel and Paul crack up. Janine watches them like she isn't sure she knows either one of them.

"I like you," Paul says. "You have the springiest, happiest hair. I wish I had happy hair. I might be happier."

"You might want to slow down on the wine there, Paul," Janine cautions.

"What about your brother? I hear he's damaged, too?"

"Bi-polar. With other stuff."

"Do you see him much?"

"No. His doc says that…well, Bruce needs a routine. A strict schedule. Changes throw him off."

"Can't you schedule time with him? See him once a week or something?"

Chantel tears up a bit. Janine grabs one of her hands, Paul the other. "I'm sorry. I didn't mean—" Paul begins.

"It's okay. I don't talk about him much…because I miss him. Even when I do see him, I miss him because he's not there, you know?"

"The meds?"

"Yeah. And the disease."

"You two were close when you were kids?"

Chantel nods and leans toward Paul. Janine recognizes that an important connection is being made, so she quietly clears the table and does the dishes while they talk. A mixture of emotions plays on her face, happiness and jealousy in turn.

"When we were kids," Chantel whispers to Paul as she holds his hand, "I used to hold his hand when he got too upset...when he got confused."

"It helped?" Paul asks.

Chantel nods. "Sometimes, we'd sit for hours, holding hands. Sometimes I'd tell him happy stories about ponies or princesses, you know, stories I thought were happy. But mostly we'd just sit together holding hands. Not even looking at each other."

HAPEVILLE

That evening, Giselle sits on the stoop of her tiny house as the sun sets in the slot between the houses across the street. She smokes a cigarette, pulling on it more agitatedly every time she checks her watch. As the top of the sun slips behind the neighbor's camellia bush, Miguel pulls up in his Lexus. He gets out slowly to piss her off, then lets Manny out of the back seat. Manny waits by the door until his dad pulls out a huge stuffed animal for him, a white dog. Manny drags it past Giselle into the house without even looking at her.

When she's sure that Manny won't hear, she glares at Miguel and says, "You're late."

Miguel holds out his hands and shrugs his shoulders, like *whatcha gonna do about it?*

"Either take him every weekend, or go the hell away. I'm tired of you breaking his heart."

"Really. Is that what you're tired of, Giselle?"

"And send the check on time, or I'm calling my lawyer."

"You do that, chica. You do that." Miguel slides his sleek body back into his expensive car and drives off. Only when Giselle hears Manny giggling and screaming in delight from inside the house does she remember Whitey.

Manny appears behind the screen door holding Whitey, who licks his face. "Mom…Whitey's here. Can he stay with us? Please?" Manny says between giggles. It's the most that Giselle has heard him say in a month. She puts a hand to her heart and is speechless. She nods and Manny runs into the living room, puts Whitey down and gets on the floor to play with him.

Giselle can't enter just yet. She watches her happy boy through the screen door.

GRANT PARK

The next morning at breakfast, Paul and Janine's table is again set for three. Paul cooks up some eggs while Janine butters the toast. Chantel comes out of the bathroom dressed in the same clothes as the night before. "Can I help?"

"No. Have a seat, girl," Paul says as he plates the eggs. Janine sits by Chantel and Paul serves three plates of eggs.

"Oh," Paul says as he sits. "Don't forget to leave that doc's card."

Chantel reaches around to grab her purse still on the back of her chair. She flips open her wallet and slides out a card. She hands it to Paul. "Dr. Ira Vlack. He has a website. You can probably e-mail him and ask."

"Ask what?" Janine says.

"If he'd do remote therapy."

"What's *remote* therapy?" Janine looks blank.

Paul and Chantel crack up. "Not *remote* therapy, remote *therapy*. So Paul can get sessions with him from home," Chantel says.

"I'll have to order a web cam. I'll check eBay today," Paul says.

"Is there anything you can't have delivered to your door?" Chantel asks.

"I was going to say new friends, but that's no longer true." Paul smiles at Chantel.

Chantel bites a piece of toast. "I've got to run and open my shop. Thanks for having me over. And letting me stay." She stands and Paul does, too. "May I?" Chantel opens her arms and Paul nods. They hug.

Janine and Chantel step into the hallway together and Janine pulls the door closed behind her.

"And thank you for sharing your bed last night," Chantel says, wrapping Janine in a lover's hug. "That was delightful." They kiss.

"You're welcome. I'm glad it turned out so…" Janine is at a loss for words.

"I know! He is such a honey. I'm glad I finally got to meet him. Gotta run." Chantel kisses Janine again, breaks away, and trots down the hallway and down the stairs. Janine watches her go.

HAPEVILLE

As Chantel puts the key into the door of the pet store, Giselle sees her and calls out good morning. Manny rushes over to Chantel with Whitey on a leash. Manny bounces off Chantel's leg, and Whitey bounces off Manny's.

"Whoa little man!" Chantel laughs.

"Whitey! He came to live—Whitey's mine—he chose me!" Manny can hardly get the words out fast enough.

"He chose well," Chantel says. "You have any questions about taking care of him, you can always stop in and ask, okay?" She bends down and pets Whitey.

Manny can't get any more words out, he just nods and nods. He and Whitey run over to the parched front yard of the beauty school and run in circles together.

"Watch out for fire ants!" Giselle calls.

"He seems to have taken it well," Chantel laughs.

"Yes. A boy and his dog," Giselle says. "Cheaper than years of therapy working through his parent's divorce."

"It's nice to see him smile."

"Yeah, I'd almost forgotten what a nice..." Giselle gets choked up and trails off. She touches Chantel's arm in thanks.

"Wait," Chantel says as she goes inside and flips on the lights in the store. Behind the counter, she pulls out a wrapped present and hands it to Giselle. "It's for Manny. A book about training puppies."

Giselle nods her thanks and walks toward the beauty school and her son.

Later that morning, as Chantel takes a fresh bowl of water to the puppies, she sees Bruce outside watching the puppies through the window. There are only five left.

Chantel gasps when she sees him, sloshing some of the water. She sets the bowl in the enclosure, strokes the beads of water off the puppies' backs, then tentatively lifts a hand to wave.

Bruce turns, gets in his car, and drives away.

FIVE POINTS

There are several attractions at the center of Atlanta. Sure, there is the Coca-Cola Museum, a monument to a product linked to cavities and obesity. There is something older there, though, called Underground Atlanta which evokes caves or an escape from slavery, though it is neither.

The original name for Atlanta was Terminus because it built up around the end of two railroad lines, the Georgia Railroad and the Western & Atlantic Railroad. When Sherman marched through and burned the city, his men were instructed to pull up the rails, heat them in large fires and then tie them into bows. It was more than the cutting off of supplies to the Confederate Army, it was his major *fuck you* to Atlanta.

In the 1920s, the city, finally fully recovered from Sherman's wrath, had traffic problems. A series of viaducts were built to elevate traffic over a portion of the downtown to relieve traffic congestion. The city lifted itself by its hooped skirts and built on the higher, viaduct level. The lower levels were sealed off and abandoned for a time. In the late 1960s, this time warp lower level was rediscovered and developed as a pot of honey to lure tourists out of the hot sun to the cooler, sunless, subterranean depths. The storefronts date from the late 1800s and early 1900s, which is incongruous with the trendy shops and restaurants and bars that now inhabit them. Sure, there's a bit of history here, but you're under the streets, pipes snake along the low ceiling, and people bump shoulders as they walk along, disoriented in the artificial light. After a few margaritas, most people feel they may be buried alive down there.

Two blocks from Underground Atlanta is the Five Points police station where Janine changes out of her uniform and into dress pants and a silk blouse. Another police woman, Diane, enters still wearing her fake hooker get-up. Diane is black, in her mid-thirties and pudgy. She tosses her wig onto the bench and sits. She pulls her swollen feet out of her platform heels and massages them.

"Hard to believe some chicks actually do this for a living," she says to Janine.

"Yeah, and you didn't even get to the blow job part of the day."

Diane makes gagging noises, and they laugh. "What a racket."

Janine smoothes her blouse and checks her reflection in the mirror.

"Hot Friday night date?"

"You might say." The smile on Janine's face fills the room with light.

"Oh, honey, that's not a hot date. That there is love."

Janine laughs and nods.

"Who's the lucky…" Diane isn't sure which pronoun to use.

"Woman. Lucky woman. Chantel. She owns a pet store. The one over in Hapeville that was robbed couple months back? Well, she's…lovely and funny and…"

"And she loves you."

Janine nods.

"Good for you, girl. True love is the bomb."

Janine looks towards the locker room door. "What about the guys?"

"Honey, you just gave a whole new dimension to their fantasies. The guys will deal!"

GRANT PARK

Paul sits at his computer. On the screen is a small window with the image of Dr. Vlack in it. Taped to the top of Paul's monitor is a new web cam.

Dr. Vlack's image moves, and he speaks. There is a slight delay between when his lips form a word and when the word is heard on the computer speakers. "Let me make sure I have all these dates correctly. First suicide attempt was as a sophomore in high school?" Paul nods. "Subsequent attempts in ninety-eight, O-one, and O-seven? Each of these with some time in an inpatient facility."

"Yes."

"And the seclusion?"

"I'd been pretty reclusive even at the conservatory."

"But the total cutting off? When was the last time you were outside your apartment complex?"

"Yeah. That. Around two years now."

"Have you applied for disability? I can assist you with that app-"

"No. I have residuals from my work. And I have a home business." Paul itches his nose with his gloved hand.

"You're supporting yourself, then?" Dr. Vlack does a double-take when he sees Paul's glove. "Do you wear the gloves constantly?"

Paul looks down at his hands. "No. No, I don't. It just felt that, well…"

"My presence here, on your screen?"

"Yes. No offense, it's like, it's like you're in my home."

"How many people do you allow to touch you? Without the gloves?"

"Just Janine."

"Your parents?"

"Mom's dead. Dad might as well be."

Dr. Vlack waits for an explanation.

"Alzheimer's. He doesn't even know who he is anymore, let alone me."

"Siblings?"

"Only child. Oh, wait, Chantel!"

"You forgot you had a sibling?"

"No. People who touch me. Janine's friend, Chantel. The woman who gave me your card. She touched my arm, even gave me a hug. The first time I met her!"

"And what is it about Chantel that you think allowed this?"

Paul thinks, then looks up from his gloved hands. "I think part of it was that she loves Janine, and I love Janine. But it was more than that. She seems like someone I've known a long time, like she knows me. And you know about her brother, Bruce, so maybe that experience somehow…maybe we recognize that damaged part of each other?"

Dr. Vlack looks up from his note taking. "Anything else?"

"No. I think that's it. Oh, her hair."

"Pardon?"

"She has the happiest hair."

Dr. Vlack stares at Paul, makes a note and continues. "Okay then, Paul. Getting back to my questions: You're able to support yourself?"

"I keep a low overhead." Paul watches Dr. Vlack's image for a look or anything to point to a sense of humor. Nothing.

"Fine. And we went over your meds, which I think are okay for now. I'd like to have a few more sessions with you before adjusting anything there, okay?"

"That sounds reasonable."

"So, Paul, what are your goals for therapy?"

Paul thinks a minute, kind of thrown by the question, the expansive sense of possibilities it calls forth. He wants to say *I want to be normal,* but thinks this may be too tall an order. "I'd like to take a walk outside," he says instead. "Maybe in front of my apartment building to start. Oh, maybe in the hallway first. The apartment hallway?"

Dr. Vlack's image looks up and into the camera. "That's a wonderful first goal, Paul," he says, writing it down.

HAPEVILLE

Giselle concludes her lesson on foil-wrapped highlights, then says, "Remember girls…" This time the entire class chimes in, "There are no ugly women, only lazy ones."

"Have a good weekend. See you all on Monday." The girls start to chat and put their notebooks away. "Remember the test Monday on highlights. Just the book test. We'll do the practical test later. And remember next Thursday we go to Friendship Village to do the old peoples' hair."

Lola and Rita groan about the test. "Why does it have to be this Monday when we got such a fierce weekend planned?" Lola says as she pulls a photo out of her notebook.

"Who's that?"

"That my Aunt Rosa."

"You ain't lying, girl, about her beauty potential bein' low," Rita says.

"And she lazy, too. Sits there on the couch all day. The couch has an Aunt Rosa shaped hole in it when she gets up. I wanted to show Teach what we're up against."

As the girls from the front of the classroom file out and Rita and Lola gather their things, Giselle looks over at Manny and Whitey asleep, curled together on the mat. The picture of contentment.

"Teach?" Lola says. Giselle turns to the girls and takes the photo from Lola's outstretched hand. "See? There are some ugly women out there. Just wanted you to know. And she the laziest person I know." Giselle doesn't argue, just hands it back to Lola.

"Have a good weekend, girls."

"Mind if we touch up before we go?" Rita asks, pointing to the make-up station with the erasable head with its style-able hair.

"Sure," Giselle says. She watches the girls add another layer of eye makeup, then line and fill their lips. The last touch is to top coat the rouge on their cheeks. The girls chatter away in rapid Spanish as they quickly go through this smooth routine. Rita re-curls her super-curled bangs and unplugs the curling iron.

"Bye, Teach!"

Giselle straightens up the room and gathers her things allowing Manny and Whitey nap a little longer. Her cell phone rings and she digs through her purse to find it. She checks the number. When she recognizes it as Miguel's, she turns her back on Manny and hisses "What?" into the phone. "How nice." Giselle walks over to the window and looks out on the fried lawn where Lola and Rita stand talking. While she listens to Miguel's excuses, the battered lawn care truck pulls up and the girls hop into the cab with Joseph.

"I would just like for Manny to have some sense of certainty and consistency in his life, that's all," Giselle whispers. "No. No, he doesn't talk about you. Not since Whitey. And you know you have to take Whitey with Manny this weekend, right? I don't think they should be apart." Giselle listens to the roar of the truck as it accelerates up the street. "Fine. See you at seven." Giselle snaps the phone closed and turns to find Manny and Whitey standing right behind her.

"Hey," she says as she bends down to him and kisses him on the head. "Good nap?" Manny nods. "Fantastic. Your dad is coming to get you and Whitey after dinner. How about we go out for pizza?"

"Fellini's?"

"Of course! That's Whitey's favorite, right?"

"Yep. 'Cause he can come with us and eat outside with us by the fountain."

"Exactly. Get Whitey's leash and let's blow this beauty school!" Giselle watches Manny and Whitey run to Manny's corner. Whitey jumps around excitedly as Manny gets the little leash. Manny turns to the puppy and firmly gives the command to sit. Whitey sits.

"He's a smart guy, isn't he?" Giselle says.

"Whitey's very smart," Manny says. "Very, very smart."

"I was talking to Whitey," Giselle jokes as she pushes Manny's thick black hair over to the side. "You, my little man, need a haircut."

"Not Lucy," Manny says.

"Promise," Giselle says. "Lucy will never again touch a hair on your head."

After dinner, Giselle, Manny and Whitey sit on the front stoop waiting for Miguel. Manny has his backpack stuffed with his things, and a smaller bag packed with Whitey's food and toys.

"Do you think Whitey will like Dad?"

"I'm sure he will. Dogs like who their masters like."

"And I'm his master, right?" Giselle nods. Manny thinks about this. "So if I don't like Dad so much, then Whitey won't, right?"

This blindsides Giselle. Before she can gather her thoughts, Miguel arrives. He parks and roars the engine once before turning it off and sliding out. Whitey stands, then Manny. Whitey moves out in front of Manny and stands his ground. A small, almost comical growl comes from the little puppy, like the dog has never tried the growl out before.

"I think you scared Whitey," Giselle says as Miguel approaches, "with the car." Miguel continues walking toward Giselle until Whitey leaps out in front of her and barks at Miguel with his yippy bark. Manny pulls on Whitey's leash until Whitey is back by his side. Manny kneels and calms the dog.

"What in the hell is that?" Miguel asks.

"This is Whitey. I told you about him on the phone."

"I thought you were talking about the stuffed dog," Miguel says, then turns to Manny. "Go get yer stuffed dog. Leave the yipper with yer mami."

Manny puts his arm around the puppy and doesn't move.

Giselle's eyes locked on Miguel's in death-ray mode. "The dog stays with Manny. Your building allows dogs, so take the dog with your son. It is important to him."

"I just got new carpet." Miguel looks down at the puppy. "Doesn't look trained yet. Maybe you can bring him this summer. We'll go up to the mountain house. He can sleep in the garage."

Manny shakes his head. Giselle walks a few steps motioning for Miguel to follow. Manny sits on the stoop,

Whitey at his side. They watch Giselle and Miguel talk in harsh whispers. Then Manny stands and the boy and his dog go back inside the house.

When Giselle comes inside, Manny is stretched out on the floor of the living room looking at a picture book. Whitey is stretched out alongside him. The boy's hands hold down one side of the book, the dog's paws hold down the other.

"Um," Giselle begins, "Your dad forgot he had a meeting this weekend." Outside, the car roars away. "So, maybe next weekend?"

Manny continues looking at the book.

"You're not upset, are you?"

Manny and Whitey both look up at her. "I'd be upset if I was with Dad," he says. And when Giselle understands this, she relaxes about trying to make peace between the boy and his father. She joins them on the floor, Whitey between her and Manny, and she looks at the book with the two of them. Manny turns the page and Whitey lifts his paws and replaces them on top of the new one.

BUCKHEAD—LITTLE FIVE POINTS

The bar crowd yells MUST BE THE MONEY to the song blasting out of the speakers encircling the dance floor. The bar is full of mostly white, young people. Most look like they are familiar with the concept of a trust fund. Joseph, Lola and Rita bob to the beat in the middle of the dance crowd, gulping their tequila shots out of plastic glasses.

"All right," the DJ says as the song fades. "Time for the ladies to chug-a-lug! Up on the bar, ladies! First one to down a beer wins! Oh, here they come, boys! Check 'em out!"

Lola and Rita lock arms and push their way through the crowd. They clamber up on the bar stools on their heels. The bartender gives them a hand to steady themselves as they climb onto the bar with the other women. He makes use of his vantage point and looks up the short skirts of the girls. He pops open bottles of beer and hands them up to all of the women.

"All right!" the DJ's voice screams out of the speakers. You must hold the empty bottle upside down over your head to show that you are finished! Ready? GO!"

Rita and Lola tip their bottles and chug away. They finish first, tied, and hold the empty bottles over their heads and scream in victory. A couple of drops of foam gather on the edge of the bottles and drop onto their hairdos.

"We have a tie! Two hot Latina mamas! We all know how much Latinas want to be mamas!!" The DJ cranks the volume on the next song as the bartender opens two more beers for the girls as their prize.

Joseph helps them down and yells into Lola's ear, "Let's go someplace else!"

"Why?" Lola yells back.

"Yeah, why?" Rita says.

"He dissed you! The DJ!" Joseph pulls Lola toward the door. Rita follows.

"Beers stay inside!" the bouncer yells at them.

"We're leaving," Joseph says. Lola and Rita chug their beers even faster than they did on the bar. They hand the empties to the bouncer and sashay past him. He watches the ruffles on their skirts flip-flap, then launches the empties into the dumpster near where Joseph and the girls are walking. They land with a smashing crash, and Joseph whirls around ready for a fight.

"Whoa, little man. No disrespect intended. Just dealing with the empties."

A second bouncer pokes his head out of the bar.

"C'mon. Let's go to that salsa club Enrico told you about," Lola pleads, pulling at Joseph's arm. Lola and Joseph stomp off toward the truck and Rita glares at the bouncers.

"Go on with your chica and her burrito, little lady. Go get y'all some salsa," the bouncer laughs. Rita gives him the finger and he says, "You wish." The inside bouncer stands shoulder-to-massive-shoulder with the outside bouncer.

"Beaners givin' you lip?"

"Nothin' I can't handle."

Rita quick-steps it to catch up to Joseph and Lola. She jumps in the cab and into their argument.

"We coulda had free beer all night!" Lola moans.

"Not free with the cover they charge," Joseph says, "and how can you put up with the looks and the fuckin' insults?"

"What? They called us 'hot Latina mamas'! Sounds like us," Lola laughs and puts her arm around Rita's shoulder. "Uh-Ha!"

Joseph pulls out of the parking lot, pushing the pedal to the rusted floor boards causing the truck to roar. "Yeah, then the asshole said that all Latinas wanted to be mamas," Joseph shouts.

"And the other bouncer called us 'Beaners,'" Rita adds when the muffler stops roaring so much.

"Jesus-n-Mary. I feel like I'm back in Mr. Garcia's class. Remember those crappy movies he showed us? How we were supposed to deal with this shit? I'm not gettin' all unsettled over someone else's ignoramus-itis. I have every right to party up in here just as much as those Georgia Tech goons and those Buckhead chicas with their money and nose jobs."

"You think that girl on the bar?" Rita asks, touching her nose.

"You know so!" Lola answers.

"Let's go to the salsa club. They play better music anyways. I'm sick of all that rap," Joseph says, heading the truck south on the highway towards downtown. A clump of tall buildings glitter ahead of them like the city of Oz. After a couple of minutes of almost unbearable thunder from the muffler as the truck struggles valiantly to reach seventy miles per hour while all other traffic races by at well over eighty, Joseph exits the highway and slows down.

"Thank Christ," Rita says, "I thought my bangs were going to go straight from all that noise. Can't you fix this truck up a bit?" She swipes her hand over the dash and looks at her palm covered with pollen and dirt. "That was a mistake," she says.

"The salsa place up in this hood?" Lola asks.

"It's in Little Five, but I wanted to show you something first." Joseph turns the truck into an entrance.

"Cartier Center," Rita reads. "Oooooo, he goin' to show us jewelry!"

"Not 'Cartier,' dippy, 'Carter,'" Joseph says, "Like the old President."

"Who you callin' dippy?" Rita says.

"Relax yourself," Lola says as they pull around the back parking lot and park. They are on a hill that looks over the downtown cluster of buildings. Joseph actually picks the exact spot where General Sherman sat his horse to watch Atlanta burn almost a century and a half ago. A full moon rises over the buildings, still low enough that it looks enormous; like it's so close it could be lassoed out of the sky. Joseph turns off the rumbling truck, puts his arm around Lola and kisses her neck.

"Oh, great. You two gonna park here and I got nobody to love on me?" Rita asks. "I thought youz gonna have one of your lawn jockies hook up with us at the bar?"

Lola and Joseph are too busy necking to answer. Rita gets out and slams the door. Chunks of rust clink onto the pavement. "I'll just take a walk around the place, okay? You two jus' keep on smacking lips. Don't worry 'bout me out here in the dark 'bout to get raped and murdered!"

Rita stomps off through the empty parking lot and the couple doesn't miss her at all; in fact, Joseph uses the extra room to recline Lola and settle himself on top of her. He moves one hand to Lola's breast, and the other to her hip. Her hands play in his hair, then slide down and grab his ass. He rubs against her as he unbuttons her blouse. He kisses the top of her breasts popping out of her tight bra and reaches around back to release them.

"Front clasp," Lola pants. This worries Joseph as he has no idea what this means or what sexual favor she might be requesting. He says something non-committal into her breasts and continues struggling to release her bra in the back. Lola grabs his thick hair and pulls his face up to her own. "The bra? It has the clasp up in the front." Joseph looks down as she demonstrates the bend and lift release on the front of the bra. She hooks it back together, and Joseph undoes it, then lays the cups to the side.

"Gloriosa," he whispers as he nuzzles and suckles. Lola moans.

Meanwhile, Rita can barely see the truck, but she can hear the squeaking of the truck springs as her friends go at it. "Not again," she says to herself. "I gotta quit bein' the add-on with those two." Rita walks downhill toward the sound of falling water. She jumps when she sees two figures up ahead, but then realizes they are statues. She gets closer, and sees that it is a statue of a boy leading a blind man.

"Mr. Cartier must be blind or somethin'," Rita mutters.

She continues toward the sound of water falling and comes through an opening in the foliage to find herself in the middle of a sloping garden ringed with Japanese lanterns. The azaleas are done blooming, but the rhododendrons still hold some of their blossoms. Rita steps over a little chain fence and down to the waterfall. She sits on the simple wooden bench there and takes a deep breath. The air is cooler here, fresher. A piece of bamboo fills with water from a smaller waterfall. When full, it tips and empties into the koi pond. When empty, it clunks back up to the beginning position and fills again. The sound it makes is calming, and the cascading water makes Rita feel that when she exhales, she is exhaling all the pent-up, exhaust-filled air that she has been holding in for years. She takes several more deep breaths to feel how large her lungs are, then she strokes the small tree near her. It is a lace maple. The leaves are soft, like fine silk, to her touch.

"Should be lepra-cons or fairies here or somethin'," Rita whispers to herself, glancing around for them. She notices the dirt from the dashboard on her hand. She rinses it off in the waterfall, shakes most of the water off and rests her hands on the back of her neck to cool down. She wonders where this place is, how it got to be so magical, and if it can really be only a few miles from the crappy neighborhood where she lives.

After a few more minutes of peace, her cell phone rings and she digs it out of her purse. "Yah-Ha? Sure you two are finished? Maybe Joe-Man wants another go? Sure? Okay, I'm comin'." She snaps her phone closed, takes one more look around, gently pulls one of the leaves off the tree and walks back to the truck, gently cupping the leaf in her hand.

GRANT PARK

D r. Vlack's voice comes out of Paul's computer speakers. His face is on the monitor. "Hello, Paul. Can you see me okay?"

Paul nods at the monitor and holds up his hands. He's not wearing gloves.

"Wonderful. That's great progress for only four sessions! How does it feel?"

"Feels okay, Doc." Paul lowers his hands onto his thighs. His white gloves are there, on top of his legs and Paul rests his hands on them.

"I'd like to talk this session about how you spend your day, okay? Moment by moment, what keeps you interested, what connections you maintain to the world. Then I'll see if we can't come up with something to help you move toward your goal."

"Sounds good, Doc."

Almost an hour into the session, Dr. Vlack learns about Paul's computer game family. "And this game takes up how much of your time each day?"

"Two, three…yes, more like three hours. Sometimes more, like if I plan to redo a room, or add onto the house. See, there are fan sites on the web where you can download things that are not in the game."

"What sorts of things?"

"Like artwork. Or special marble tiles. Or custom furniture."

Dr. Vlack studies Paul's face, waiting for more.

"It would be like if you could only shop at the local furniture store, then all of a sudden someone took you to Ikea."

"Did you have a desire to visit Ikea? The new one here in town?"

"I've seen their catalog."

"Do you care to go?"

"I'm fine with their catalog."

"I'm asking if that could be a future goal?" Paul begins to shake. Dr. Vlack notices, and backs off. "Paul…Paul. Let's return to talking about your computer game. Focus on the game for a moment if you will."

"I really prefer to call them my family."

"Right. Your family." He makes a note. "What are their names?"

"Well, one of the men is me. Paul."

Later, Paul plays with his computer family. Classical music fills the entire apartment from speakers in the living room. On the computer, Paul adds a tall, brick wall around his family's large backyard. Paul's breathing is irregular as he does this and sweat runs down his face. It is as if he, himself, is stepping outside. When the last section of the wall is finished, he relaxes by the slightest of degrees. He pulls down the menu to add a swimming pool.

The apartment door opens and closes.

"Paul?" Janine says from the other room. "Are you here?"

"Yes," Paul shouts over the music, then, softer, "where else would I be?"

Janine enters and stands behind him. She heard his remark. "It's just a greeting…" Janine looks at the computer screen. She puts her hands on Paul's shoulders and squeezes slightly. "You're outside. Oh my god. You're outside."

BUCKHEAD

Janine and Chantel share the same winged chocolate dessert that Janine had at this restaurant with her mother. They attack it from two sides and have their free hands entwined on the booth between them.

Chantel takes another bite and swoons.

"Didn't I tell you?" Janine smiles.

"You didn't say dark chocolate, though. It's all dark!"

An air of bliss envelops them.

A woman, Vanessa, is about to shatter it. She steams across the restaurant toward the lovers. Vanessa is Latina, in her early fifties, but making every effort to seem younger including stuffing herself into a trendy dress meant for a woman in her twenties.

"Janine? Janine! I thought that was you, girl!"

Janine withdraws her hand from Chantel and scoots slightly away from her. Chantel puts down her fork and watches Janine interact with this woman.

"Vanessa. How nice—"

Vanessa leans down and air-kisses Janine, ignoring Chantel.

"This is Chantel," Janine says, "My…friend."

"Hey-ya," Vanessa waves at Chantel without looking at her. "Did your mother tell you about Miguel? The man who just moved into the condos? He is *fine*! And doesn't have his kid much, maybe every third weekend! I haven't seen him around in awhile. Little boy. Seems nice, though. Quiet." She glances at Chantel and keeps steamrolling. "Not like the brats you see in most divorces. This little man—I think his name is Manny—he's so quiet and respectful! Proper! Mm, hmmm! And Miguel is a sight in his swim trunks. Cut!" Vanessa motions with her hands from her hips to her groin. "You know that 'HE-VEE' muscle men get? Well, girl, he GOT! I tell you," Vanessa gives Janine a critical once over, "you better drop a couple of pounds—girl, do that hot pepper cleanse!—get a bikini wax, and get on over before one of your Mother's friends snaps him up! She's holding us off, but you know that can only work for so long!"

"Right, well I..." Janine attempts while Vanessa takes a singular breath.

"See you at the pool, girl!" Vanessa turns and totters away on her heels. "Nice to meet you, Chanel," she tosses over her shoulder.

The quiet between Janine and Chantel grows oppressive. Neither one of them can focus on the dessert anymore.

"Chantel," Chantel whispers to herself.

"What?"

"My name. Chantel. That woman called me Chanel."

"That woman...is an ass," Janine says. This cuts the tension a little. "She's a friend..."

"Of your mother?"

"Yes."

"That explains some of it. So, when are you going to meet this hunky guy?"

Janine moves to hold Chantel's hand, but she moves both of her hands to her coffee cup.

"You know I'm not. You know I'm with you."

"Do I?"

"It's just..."

"Mother Dearest?"

Janine nods and studies the table cloth. "Can I take some time with that? Just about everyone else knows." She looks at Chantel. "Does your brother know?"

"If Bruce was stable, I'd tell him."

"I know. I'm just saying that family is a different level and I need some time with that level. Otherwise, I'm yours, and I love you. So, embrace that."

Chantel motions to their waiter. "I think we need the check. I sense a night of embracing ahead."

HAPEVILLE

Bruce parks his sedan outside the pet store and gets out. He walks up to the window. There is only one puppy left now, a black one, the runt of the litter. It is curled and sleeping in the corner all alone. Bruce splays his calloused hands on the glass, then presses his nose against the window. The puppy wakes and sees him, walks to the window and wags his tail. Bruce waves to the little puppy and the puppy's tail wags even faster. Bruce moves toward the door and enters the pet store.

At the window display, he gently lifts the puppy. He cuddles him against his broad chest, turns and sees Chantel.

"How much is this puppy in the window?"

Chantel chuckles at this and walks toward him. "Hello, Bruce."

"Hello, Chantel. How much is my puppy?"

"Oh, Bruce. You can't care for a puppy. You can barely care for yourself."

"You don't know me."

Chantel gasps. "Bruce, I've known you my whole life."

"I'm getting better. Doc Vlack put me on a new med. Better meds."

Chantel holds out her hands, wanting to embrace him, but instead says, "Give me the puppy."

"I have money. I want to buy my puppy." The puppy yips and licks Bruce's face.

"You can't take a puppy into the house, Bruce."

"Why?"

"The papers. There's no room."

"I'll get rid of them. Clean them all out."

This shocks Chantel. "You do that…you show me, and I'll give you the puppy."

Bruce reluctantly hands him back. He leaves the store. Outside, he stops and yells through the window, "Don't sell my puppy to anyone but me!"

The puppy hasn't taken his eyes off Bruce. At the sound of his voice, the puppy yips and wags his tail like crazy. Chantel looks at the puppy's reaction. "You know that guy? That's my brother, that guy."

Chantel puts the puppy back into the window display and watches Bruce's olive sedan disappear up the street. She watches even after it is no longer visible, then she looks down at the puppy and sees that he, too, is still looking up the road. Chantel walks to the check-out counter, pulls out a piece of paper and a fat black marker. She slowly writes 'SOLD' on the paper, walks over and tapes it to the interior of the puppy display.

GRANT PARK

In the basement of the junior high school, Bruce feeds bundles of newspapers into the incinerator. The light from the flames splashes on his face. The trash room is crowded with many more stacks to burn.

At Bruce's house, the stacks of papers, over many, many days, dwindle and disappear until the morning sun can stream freely through the windows. The shafts of light are unimpeded and glorious, twinkling, alive with constellations of dust.

A few blocks away, Paul sits at his computer designing the backyard for his family. There is now an elaborate pool with a diving board. There is a patio area with lush plantings and chaise lounges and a grill.

Paul installs a fountain in the corner of the walled area and surrounds it with flowering plants and potted topiaries. He pulls his viewpoint back to see both the interior of the house and the backyard. His computer family, the two loving men and their two happy children, stand at the back wall of the house which is now floor to ceiling glass panes. They look out at the backyard. Pulling further back, it is clear that there are no doors at all in the exterior walls of their house. The simulated family is trapped inside, exactly like Paul.

Paul pulls down a menu and selects a beautiful set of French doors. His whole body begins to shake. He clicks on it, but cannot install it. He saves the game and turns off his monitor. He holds his head in his hands and shakes all over, gasping for breath, gasping.

Later that day, Paul listens to FOUR SONGS OF YEATS. He stands in his boxers again, directing the modern and spirited arrangement with syncopated percussion. There is an excited, contented smile on his face as his upper body flows with the music and the floating voice of the soprano.

In the hallway, Ken stands holding two bags of groceries. He sets them down on a large UPS box from "The Body Shop" and is about to do his special knock, but hears the music coming from the apartment. He pushes the box against the wall and sits with his back against it, content to listen. He pulls a folded piece of paper out of his back pocket and a nub of a pencil and begins to sketch.

About a mile away at Millie's Diner, Lorraine stands at the counter, waiting for Millie to empty her pockets of all their money. Lorraine raps her flawless acrylic nails on the counter, glaring at Millie's back as she pours herself a cup of coffee.

"I'd love a cup, Mama!" Lorraine chirps sarcastically, "Thanks for asking!" She gracefully slides onto one of the stools at the counter.

Millie pours a second cup of coffee. When it is almost full, she carefully spits in it so that Lorraine doesn't see. She shuffles over to the counter and sets the sloshing cup of hot coffee in front of Lorraine. Lorraine pulls back, makes sure that Millie didn't get any coffee on her flower skirt, and blots the spilled coffee with a napkin. "I would say thank you, but, you know."

Millie grunts and starts digging through her apron for the money. Lorraine sips the coffee, grimaces and sets it aside. "I don't know how you stay in business, Mama," Lorraine mutters.

Millie pulls up a handful of bills and coins and piles it on the counter near her. She glares at Lorraine.

"I don't have all day now, Mama." Lorraine reaches for the money and Millie blocks her with her saggy forearm. "Now, Mama, we have a legal, binding arrangement."

"Civil court judgment, more like. 'Cause you couldn't get no criminal charges to stick, girl."

"Be that as it may." Lorraine reaches for the money once more.

"Until?"

"Until what?"

"When does it end, Lorraine?"

"Why, that's a long ways off, Mama."

"Not by my accounting." Millie wads up five singles and tosses them one at a time at Lorraine. They bounce off her bosom and onto the counter. She slides several coins across the scuffed formica. Millie swipes the rest of the money back into her apron. She stands as tall as her curved back will allow and glares at Lorraine.

"It can't possibly…"

Millie reaches under the counter and pulls out a coffee-stained ledger. She slams it on the counter and grabs

Lorraine's cup, sloshing coffee on the coins and wadded bills.

"I don't want to see your face. Ever again." With that, Millie takes the cup into the kitchen.

Lorraine sits, stunned, then blots the money dry. She smoothes the bills and stacks the coins—exactly five dollars and sixty-six cents—and puts it into her canvas pouch. She opens the ledger. Fifty thousand dollars is written in large red numbers on the first yellowed and stained page. There is a string of very small subtractions from this amount on page after page. The pages get less worn and stained as she flips through them. The last page with writing on it has the bold figure of five dollars and sixty-six cents circled in red.

The judgment against Millie has been paid.

Lorraine is stunned.

A t Paul's apartment building, Ken still sits in the hallway. He's sketched a rather abstract basket form on the paper while enjoying one of Paul's beers. He stops to study the sketch as the music from inside the apartment stops. He gets to his feet and raps on the door four times. There are two raps from within, and Ken answers with two more raps.

The door opens on the chain, revealing a slice of Paul's face through the gap.

"Hey," Ken says, "got yer groceries."

"Thanks."

"Can I ask you something?" He waits for Paul to answer, but he doesn't. "Well, what was that? Playing? I don't know the composer."

Paul shakes a bit, but he smiles. "Yes. You do know the composer." Ken looks puzzled. "I wrote that," Paul clarifies.

"I liked it."

"Thanks."

"Can I get a copy of it somewhere? Is it, like, for sale?"

"It is, but I'll make you a copy."

"Sure, okay. Thanks." The door begins to close. "Wait. Where did you study?"

"Curtis."

"Philly?"

Paul nods, gasps. "Studied with Ned Rorem. Have to go now."

"Okay."

The door closes. Ken looks down at the groceries and pulls out another beer so as not to leave Paul with an odd number. Ken leaves with the bottles, without having been paid for the delivery. Inside the apartment, Paul slumps to the floor, exhausted from the effort of communicating with someone on the outside.

HAPEVILLE

That night, Bruce stands at the window of the pet store, visiting his puppy like he has every night since first holding him. The puppy watches every move he makes. Bruce takes a note from his pocket and reads it over again. Satisfied, he carefully folds it and wedges it in the store door. He waves goodbye to his puppy and drives off into the night.

The next day when Chantel unlocks the front door, Bruce's note falls to the ground. She picks it up and smoothes it on the counter. It says: "House clean. I'm ready for Puppy to come home. Come by today at one to see."

Janine enters the store from the outside; her police cruiser is parked at the curb. Chantel looks up from the note. "Hi."

"Hi," Janine answers. "Everything okay?"

"Yeah." Chantel folds the note.

"Do you want to do lunch today?"

"Can't. Sorry."

"Okay. I forgot something upstairs."

"Better not be your gun, you know I hate havin' that thing around here," Chantel teases. Janine spins around at the foot of the stairs and puts her hand on her gun like an outlaw ready to draw. Chantel laughs and watches her go up the stairs. She stuffs the note into her pocket. Janine comes back down and walks up to her.

"I'll see you tonight then?" Janine asks.

Chantel nods, and Janine leans over the counter and kisses her gently, lingeringly. Chantel watches her get into her police cruiser and drive away.

Chantel checks her schedule of things to do in the store and sees that it is the day to clean the fish tanks. This is the task she likes the least, and she wonders, again, why she even stocks the fish when she, herself, has no affection for them. She starts to walk to the back room when the bell on the front door rings. Giselle pops her head into the store, then leans back out to yell to Manny, "Give the man his pastry, Manny. Wake him gently." She pops her head back inside and asks, "Are you okay?"

"Yeah. Why?"

"The police car. Thought you had more trouble?"

"No," Chantel grins. "I'm dating the cop that wrote up the break-in."

"So that's what it takes to meet someone? I gotta be a crime victim?" Giselle and Chantel laugh together. "She's cute. Oh, here." She hands a novel to Chantel. "Thanks. I loved it! Pick another for me!"

"Sure."

Giselle glances outside again. "Gotta run," she says as she hurries next door.

Twenty minutes later, Lola and Rita rush by the store, late for class. They yell a greeting and Chantel waves to them. The girls stop on the front porch of the school to catch their breath. Rita looks in the window and says, "We're the first ones. We got a minute." They sit on the front step.

"So why you doin' this?" Lola asks.

"Marta runs to it and I got to get me a better job to pay Teach for the beauty lessons."

"But why there? Why don't chu ask Chantel if she need you to watch the pet store? You could play with the bunnies and puppies."

"Yeah, that'd be nice, but I want to check out that Cartier Center. See what goes on there." Rita pulls the faded lace maple leaf out of her notebook and strokes it. "I went to their website and they have places to eat in there and they cater sometimes and they have a gift shop, so I'm thinking I can get a job at one of those places, figure out what all goes on there, and move up the ladder."

"What ladder? You don't like heights, girl!"

"The employment ladder," Rita snorts.

"What about hair? Makeup? Ya'll know we the best students up in this here school."

"We only got two months left, Lola. I can always do hair. I just want to see if there's something more for me somewheres else."

"Yeah, but why up in that Carter Center? Looks all weird. The buildings look like spaceships that landed or something."

"I can't explain it. It gives me a feeling inside. All peaceful and—"

"Hey-ya!" the other students say as they walk across the front yard to the school. Giselle pokes her head out the door and scowls. They all hurry inside for class.

GRANT PARK

Paul puts a blank CD into the computer drive and clicks the mouse a few times to copy files to the disc. While it copies, Paul pulls a few stray dead leaves from the vibrant plants on his windowsill. He mists them and hums a tune. The largest plant in the center of the sill is a lush, variegated spider plant. Its babies spill over the sill, cascading down the wall and puddling on the floor. He takes extra time with this plant, murmuring to it. When the CD drive opens, Paul puts down the misting bottle, takes out the CD and places it into a holder. He pulls a sheet out of the printer and trims it to fit inside. It says: "Four Songs of Yeats" by Paul Shipley.

Paul walks the CD to the desk by the apartment door and places it there. He pulls out a pair of gloves from the drawer and puts them next to the CD. Then, he scoots the desk a couple of feet away from the door. Then, he sits and waits.

A few blocks away, Chantel parks her car. She gets out and looks up the slight hill to the tired old house, her childhood home with Bruce. The house is more visible now that the riot of spring blooms has died off. Memories wash over her face. She walks slowly up the front steps. She touches the old wooden door and the brass knocker.

She raps on the door twice and steps back. Bruce opens the door and Chantel steps into the large living room. It is now empty except for the old couch and coffee table and a small stack of newspapers on the floor in a corner. The place is incredibly dusty, but it has been cleaned out.

Bruce waves his arm to indicate all the empty space. "See? Okay?" Chantel looks at the small stack of newspaper still left. "I kept some papers for training him. They say to let them pee on the papers."

Chantel moves to the coffee table and looks from Bruce to the two medicine bottles. She's looking for permission to study them, but he doesn't give it. He's focused on getting his puppy. Chantel gathers the bottles anyway and looks at the names. She points to the larger of the bottles. "Is this the new one? Does it help?"

Bruce nods. "I'm not seeing stuff that isn't there anymore."

She sets them all back down. "And the doc thinks you're ready for a pet?"

"Yes."

"What about the weekends, Bruce? When you work?"

"I can take him with me."

"Are you sure?"

Bruce nods. "I called my supervisor."

"You called him? On the telephone?"

"Yeah."

"You never call."

"It was hard, but not as hard this time. I hung up the first time I got his machine. Then I wrote it out on paper. What to say. So it wouldn't be so hard."

Chantel looks around the room. It is filled with so many memories. "I haven't been in here since Mama died. Long time."

Bruce looks impatient. "I'll go back with you. To the store. To get him."

Chantel looks down the straight hallway to the kitchen at the back of the house, and out the window in the back door.

"Okay?" Bruce asks.

"What?"

"Puppy. I'll come and get him."

"Oh. He's here." Bruce looks blankly at Chantel. "Out in a box in my car. I brought your puppy with me."

"You knew I'd be ready."

"I had hoped, Bruce. I have never lost that for you." Her voice catches. "The hope." She moves toward the front door, opens it. Bruce walks outside and stops on the porch. "Can I visit you? And the puppy?" Chantel asks.

Bruce doesn't answer, he doesn't hear her, he only has eyes for his puppy jumping in the back of Chantel's car, his head popping briefly above the level of the box so he can get high enough to see Bruce.

Back at the apartment, Paul still sits. The CD for Ken still on the desk.

Paul is waiting.

He is exceptionally good at waiting.

Paul hears something in the hall. He slips on the gloves as the footsteps stop at his door. Grocery bags rustle. There are four soft knocks and Paul answers with two, then opens the door on the chain. He peers out at a slice of Ken through the gap.

"Dude! You didn't let me do my answer knock!"

"Yeah. It's okay. I heard the bags. I knew it was you." Paul slides the CD through the opening. Ken takes it, careful not to touch Paul's gloves.

"Thanks. I'm honored. This is FIERCE!"

"Um, do you know 'Sister Angelica'?"

"Dude," Ken says. "I'm not even Catholic."

Paul actually smiles at this.

"What?"

"By Puccini? 'Sister Angelica' by Puccini."

"Oh. No. Can't say as I do."

"It's my favorite opera. Ever." Paul begins to sweat from the effort of this conversation, but he presses onward. "Do you have time? To listen with me?"

Ken knows this is huge for Paul. He doesn't even glance at his watch. "Sure, dude." He waits for the door to open, but Paul pushes a button on a remote control and the opera begins to play. Paul sits in the space he made between the desk and the door with his back against the inside wall of the apartment. Ken watches this then he sits with his back against the partially opened door, but not too close to the opening. They can see slices of each other through the chained gap.

The opera begins softly in the background with church bells, then an angelic choir singing in Italian. A flute plays over the choir and a soprano begins to sing.

"Angelica was from a rich family," Paul says through the crack in the door. "She got pregnant out of wedlock." They listen for a few moments as the choir gets louder. "Her family took her son away to raise him and sent her to the convent." Paul is calm and coherent when talking about the opera. This is the one arena where he approaches normalcy.

Ken listens to the soaring notes of the soprano. "Is that Renee Fleming?"

"No. Lucia Popp. Don't you love her voice?"

"Yeah. So, what happens next?"

"Listen," Paul says. He puts his head against the wall and does more than listen. It's like he absorbs the music, the singing, the arias, the life from the opera. He fills with it.

Ken closes his eyes and listens, too.

Almost an hour later, they are still there, listening to the climax of the opera. Both men have tears in their eyes.

The soprano sings, almost gasps, "Madonna! Madonna!"

Paul whispers into the gap. "Sister Angelica drinks the poison, then walks to the Madonna. The Madonna holds her dead son. The son she could not be with in life, she joins in death."

The soprano gasps two magnificent notes, "Ah! Ah!" There is a heavenly chorus as Sister Angelica dies. The music ends.

The men sit in silence for a moment. Ken pulls himself together. "Dude," he says, "That is the saddest thing I've ever heard."

They continue to sit together, looking in opposite directions, in different rooms, but still, despite this, finally, firmly, friends.

HAPEVILLE

That evening, above the pet store, Chantel stirs dinner at the stove in the tiny kitchen. She glances over at Janine who sits on the bed, talking on the phone.

"Hey. Paul." Janine says into the phone. "I'm at Chantel's. Just wanted to check in with you." She smirks. "No, you're not my parent. I wanted—I haven't been home much, and, well—" Janine pushes her hair back. "Okay. As long as you're okay." She nods again. "I'll tell her."

Janine hangs up, the goes to Chantel. She embraces her gently from behind. "Paul says 'hi.'"

"He doing okay?"

"Yes."

"We should do dinner over your place again. I like Paul."

"He likes you, too."

Chantel focuses on stirring the dinner, pulling slightly away from Janine.

"Hey," Janine says. "It's okay if you don't want to talk about whatever you're thinking about." Chantel nods at this. "I want you to know that I'm here, though, okay?" Chantel continues stirring. Janine embraces her again, closer this time, kissing her on the nape of her neck.

"I saw the last puppy sold today. When do we get the next litter? I already miss the little guys."

Chantel shrugs and keeps stirring.

Janine embraces her tighter.

Chantel looks surprised. "Is your gun in your pocket?"

"No. I'm just...glad to see you?"

Chantel reaches a hand around and feels the front of Janine's pants. "I didn't think you wanted—"

"I thought we could, maybe try—you said—?"

"Where'd you?"

"We padlocked the sex shop over on King Street today."

Chantel turns around within Janine's arms.

"It was new. Still in the package."

"Okay."

"And it…"

"What?"

"It glows in the dark."

"Do tell." Chantel turns off the stove and gives her full attention to Janine and the new toy in her pants.

The next morning, Janine is dressed in her police uniform. She quietly pads over to the bed holding her boots and sits there to put them on. Chantel rolls toward her and rubs Janine's back.

"Mornin' sunshine."

Janine leans over and kisses her. "Coffee's on. Want me to bring you a cup?"

"That's okay. I'll get it."

"Did you have fun last night?" Janine asks.

"I always have fun with you."

"I mean, with the…"

"Oh. I'm not sure it was…" Chantel squints, "… necessary?"

"Do you prefer—"

"Either. Neither. I'm not…"

"It's okay. Either way with me, too."

"Oh. I thought you—"

"Kind of. Maybe once in a while," Janine mutters.

Chantel fingers Janine's shiny belt buckle, then glances up at the badge pinned to her shirt. "Can we talk about this when you're not in uniform? I have that whole…"

"…trouble with authority?"

"Thing. Yeah."

"Sure. See you tonight." Janine kisses her, momentarily playing with one of the springs of hair on Chantel's head. "Maybe we can do dinner with Paul this Saturday?" Chantel nods.

Janine leaves, down the stairs and out through the pet store.

LITTLE FIVE POINTS

R ita sits at a table in the café at The Carter Center. She glances around as she fills out the job application in front of her. She signs the bottom of the paper and flips the application over. It is blank on the backside, so she takes it to a black woman refilling the coffee carafes.

"Do I leave this here with y'all?" she asks the woman.

"What? Sure, hon. Just set it on the tray rail and I'll take it back to the office when I'm done here."

Rita sets the application down, but doesn't leave.

"Somethin' else, hon?"

"Just wonderin' when I can expect to hear from you."

"You in some kind of rush to work in a café, girlie?"

"I am in some kind of rush to work in this here center, ma'am."

"You feel some sort of attachment to a President who served before you were even born?"

This stumps Rita. She is only thinking of the garden and the falling water and the calm she felt. "Yes ma'am," she says.

"That's refreshing. A young person who knows Mr. Carter's work, his ongoing legacy. Have you toured the museum?"

"Not in a long time," Rita says, figuring this is not a lie because never is, indeed, a long time.

"You stay here then. I'll go on back and get you a pass from the office." The woman picks up the application. "And I'll put this on the top of the pile, Miss..." she scans the form, "Miss Rita. Have yourself some coffee in the meanwhile."

The woman waves the application in the air like a flag and strolls back to the kitchen area. Rita looks out into the

large lobby of the museum. A bronze bust of Jimmy Carter
is on display and Rita studies it across the distance. She
pumps herself a cup of coffee and sips while she gazes at
the gentle kindness on Carter's carved face.

Later on, Rita makes her way slowly through the museum,
reading each plaque, longing to touch everything,
especially the formal wear of Rosalynn Carter. At one point,
when there isn't anyone around, she leans over the velvet
rope and ever-so-gently glances her finger tips against
the fine silk and lace on the gown Rosalynn wore to the
inaugural ball.

At that moment, her phone rings and she jumps, then
snaps it open. "Yeah?!" She nods her head. "I am up at the
Carter Center. I told you my plans for this Saturday, Lola!"
She pulls the phone away and scowls at it, then brings it
back to her ear. "Well, I *was* serious! And I am here learning
everything I can about President Mr. Jimmy Carter and his
wife Mrs. Rosalynn Carter and their daughter Miss Amy
Carter!" Rita walks a bit more, then hisses into the phone, "I
told you this was important to me, Lola. Oh, look, there's his
round office!! Got to go!" Rita closes the phone and pushes
the button on the wall. Jimmy Carter's recorded voice comes
out of the speakers and he talks about the oval office and his
presidential term. Rita listens, enthralled.

Later, Rita walks outside and makes her way back to the
Japanese Garden. She steps over the chain and sits on the
simple bench where she sat before. In the daylight, it is clear
that this is a restricted area. Rita thinks about everything
she saw on display inside, especially about all the good that
President Carter is still doing in the world. It amazes her
that he even won a gold medal for his work, the Nobel Peace
Prize. She imagines him up on a tri-tiered riser, like in the
Olympic ceremony, Carter on the very highest platform in
the center, with, maybe, two other lesser presidents on the

other levels—like Clinton and Bush—and President Carter gets the gold medal! How she would have cheered for him!

Rita has never been much into politics, or even much into the Olympics until they came to Atlanta when she was little, but President Jimmy Carter and his Carter Center has awakened something in her and she wonders exactly what it is and where it will take her. She reaches down and touches the top of the water with her fingers.

"You can't sit there," a low voice startles her and she turns expecting to see President Carter. A security guard stands on the other side of the low chain.

"There's a little bench here, so why can't I sit," Rita counters when she sees the skinny security guard who is about her age.

"The Japanese garden isn't open to the public, Miss."

"I'm not the public, Mister. I am an employee of the Carter Center." Rita says this thinking it isn't really a lie because she's just about hired and she feels like she belongs here.

"Oh," the guard looks at her again in her short skirt and sleeveless blouse and is not quite convinced that she can be in a pay grade that is allowed to use the garden. He needs this job, though, and doesn't want to piss off anyone who can get him fired. "Sorry, Miss. I didn't see your badge."

Rita turns away from him so he can't see that she doesn't have a badge, and he tromps up the path to continue his rounds of the thirty-acre grounds of the Center. "I'll let it go this time," she calls after him, then snickers to herself. She takes deep breaths of the calm, humid air and feels like she is growing and growing and growing.

GRANT PARK

Janine clears the dinner dishes, while Paul and Chantel chat.

"Dr. Vlack is great. He's got me setting goals and working toward certain things with my fam...i...ly..." Paul trails off and looks panicked toward Janine.

She shakes her head. "I didn't tell her," she says.

Chantel glances between Janine and Paul. "What? It's cool. I have strange family, too."

Janine chuckles. "Not as strange as Paul's." Janine begins rinsing the dishes at the sink, her back to the other two.

"You don't have to talk about it," Chantel says.

"No. It's okay." He looks at her. "Do you play computer games?"

"No, all that shooting and stuff. Doesn't do much for me."

Paul shakes his head. "Not those games. This one is a simulation game."

"What does it simulate?"

"Life," Paul answers. "People. Living. In houses with furniture with their families. With meals and dishes and bathroom breaks. And pajamas and bedtime, night and day."

"And you watch them?"

"Kind of. You're also kind of like a god, giving them new furniture or a television or a new wing on their house. And you help them to get along and take care of each other. On the computer."

"Do they talk to you?"

"They have a language that has the same inflection as English...and some of the same words, but, no, they don't speak to me directly." Paul's eyes light up. "Like when one of the dads makes dinner, one of the kids might eat some of it and say '*This frau is frekenshea!*' Which means something like '*This casserole is GREAT!*' So, you kind of know what they're saying. And they have contentment meters that float over their heads."

Chantel looks blankly at Paul. Janine clears the rest of the dishes between them. She smirks at Paul as she does this.

"Well," he explains, "like right now? The meter over my head would be full and green, meaning I'm happy to be with friends after a good meal."

"So you can always tell how they're doing?" Chantel asks.

"Yes."

"Well, that would be helpful in real life," Chantel says, glancing over at Janine.

Paul nods. "So, anyway, Dr. Vlack has me designing a backyard for my family to, like, get me outside in a virtual world before I venture into the real world."

"Very cool."

Paul locks eyes with Chantel. "Thanks. I wasn't sure I could explain it so it wouldn't sound...creepy."

"I get it. People make their pets part of their family all the time. You have a virtual family that you care for."

"Yeah. And I'm allergic."

"To a real family?"

"Pets," Paul laughs. "Cats mostly, but dogs, too."

"Did you have any pets growing up?"

"Fish," Paul says.

Together, Paul and Chantel say, "I hate fish." They dissolve into laughter and Janine turns and stares at them.

"Though I put a water feature that runs into a koi pond in the backyard I'm making for my family. And I was able to find a site that sells ferns for the game, so I have a waterfall that runs down the length of the wall, cascading over boulders, down to an expansive koi pond. I put hanging ferns on the wall, moss on the rocks, and I'm doing elaborate plantings around the pond." He looks over at Janine. "I've looked all over for a spider plant like Bartholomew, but there aren't any. I'm going to design one and put it on my site." Chantel looks questioningly at Paul and he continues. "I have a website that sells things for the houses—like art and cool rugs that I design with a graphics program. I didn't think about adding plants until I started on my backyard. It's a whole new field!"

"So to speak…" Chantel smiles.

"Ha! Field! Plants! Ha!" Paul says.

"Do you make money on that site, or is it like—" Chantel asks.

"Oh no, he makes real cash with that site," Janine interjects. "Serious cash."

"Ever seen the Japanese garden at the Carter Center?" Chantel asks.

Paul shakes his head.

"You can go online and check it out. They may even have web cams there. A master Japanese gardener designed it. It has a waterfall and a koi pond, like what you're doing. It's a lovely place. So…tranquil."

Paul nods. "I'll check it out. Thanks."

Janine wipes her hands on a dishtowel and walks closer to the table. "How about a game?"

"Blockus!" Paul says.

"Sure. I don't know it, but—" Chantel says.

"It's easy," Paul assures her.

Later, during the third game of Blockus, Chantel studies the board, then clicks down one of her blue pieces. "Ha! Cut you off!" she says in triumph to Janine.

"I thought you'd never played this before," Janine says as she takes a very small green piece and tries to fit it somewhere, anywhere, on the board.

"I haven't. It's fun, though."

"Fun when you don't lose three games in a row," Janine mutters as she sets her piece down on the table in defeat.

"It's me and you now, Paul," Chantel says.

Paul grins back and holds up one of his red pieces. He clicks it into place and says, "Take that!"

Janine stands, grabs the coffee carafe and brings it over to the table. She pours some into her own cup, and says, "Coffee?"

Paul and Chantel stare at the board, then lock eyes with each other. "So, it's gonna be like that, huh?" Chantel says to Paul.

"Yeah. It's gonna be like that," he answers as he twirls his next piece.

Chantel looks at her few remaining pieces, then back at the board.

"Coffee? No, thank you," Janine mutters as she replaces the carafe on the counter. She slumps back into her chair and holds her coffee mug as she watches the war between her lover and best friend.

"I won a game, and you won a game, Chantel, so don't blow this move," he taunts her.

"Not that there's any pressure..." she taunts back.

"No. No pressure at all." Paul holds up his last two pieces which are considerably smaller than Chantel's remaining pieces.

"Too bad," she says, "because I LOVE pressure!" She clicks her largest piece onto the board.

Paul stares with disbelief. "How'd you? What?"

"It's called 'skill,' Paul."

"Is that what it's called?"

"I do believe that's what it's called."

Paul clicks down his second to last piece. "So this would be called a 'SKILLFUL' move, right?"

Chantel studies the board as she holds her last piece. "Yes, but not as skillful as this move, BAM!" she shouts as she places it on the board. "Oh, look at that? No more blue pieces! Guess that means I won!"

Paul studies the board and places his tiny red piece in an almost impossible place. "Guess it's more like a tie, girl."

"No way!"

"Way! It happens sometimes when another player goes out early." They look at Janine.

"You're welcome," Janine says sarcastically. She watches as Paul and Chantel crack up together.

"It's like you two are high when you're together. I should bust you both for having too good a time!"

Chantel and Paul look at each other conspiratorially, then, at the same time, go at Janine saying, "Someone needs a hug!" Janine play-fights them off, then gets pissed and backs away from them stiff-armed. She grabs her leather jacket off the chair and twists the door knob.

"Just stay the hell away," she sputters. She leaves, slamming the door behind her.

Chantel looks at Paul. "Do you listen? Or do you go after her?"

Paul smirks. "Well, I usually wait for her to come back home, but, you know, that's *me*."

Chantel stares at the door for a moment longer, then looks at Paul and gets it. She chuckles. "What's going on with our girl?"

"She ever like this when it's just you two?"

Chantel shakes her head. "When she's with you?" Paul shakes his head. "So it's me and you together, right?"

"She's not good at sharing," Paul says, "never was. That's why I'm the perfect best friend, locked away alone where she always knows where I am."

"Until I came here," Chantel says and Paul nods. "How do we fix this?"

"We don't. She has to figure it out."

"Should I stop coming over?" Chantel asks.

"That would be," Paul searches for the best words, "a real loss, wouldn't it?"

Chantel nods. "But maybe for a while? Until she gets her head on straight?"

"Oh, sure," Paul smirks, "let the terrorists win!"

Chantel cracks up with him and puts an arm around his shoulders. "You're too funny to stay cooped up in here all the time. Tell Dr. Vlack to get on the stick so we can meet for lunch dates or something, okay?"

"Will do," Paul says, but he pulls away from Chantel's half-embrace and begins packing up the game.

VIRGINIA-HIGHLANDS—GRANT PARK

L orraine stands opposite the bank teller. The counter between them is strewn with the stained bills and coins she last got from Millie. Lorraine pulls out a check from Social Services and places it on top of the messy currency. Her hands shake.

"Now, I will wait until you provide me with a print out," Lorraine says in a barely controlled voice.

The teller nods, but says, "That may take a while, Lorraine. We may not even be able to go back that far. You're talking over a decade, and well—"

"It is imperative that you go back the full sixteen years. I have been with this bank for longer than that. You should be able to give me documentation of our fiduciary relationship." As Lorraine leans menacingly across the pile of cash, her breasts push some of the bills into the lap of the teller.

"If you are going to get mean, Lorraine, I will have you speak with the manager."

Lorraine loses it, slaps the counter with both hands, sending cash and checks flying as she screams, "Then call the fucking manager! Do it! Call him! The fucking manager! Do it! Call him now!"

The teller scuttles toward the manager's office.

T hat evening in the Highlands, the music from inside a hip dance club thump-thumps its way into the cool night. The line to get into this city hot-spot is comprised of straight couples and groups of friends mixed in with the men couples and women holding hands. It all seems pretty harmonious. Chantel joins the back of the line and looks up and down the street.

A t the same time in Grant Park, Bruce walks through the living room toward the front door. His footsteps echo in the open space. He stops and his puppy scurries over to him and sits at his feet.

"Yep. Time to go to work again."

The puppy's tail wags like crazy. Bruce squats down and the puppy leaps into his arms. As the puppy licks him, a broad grin slowly transforms the night janitor's face.

Chantel still stands in the line for the club. It has grown behind her. She looks around the street again, and frowns at her watch. When she looks up, Janine stands there at her side.

"Oh! Hi!" Chantel says. "I wasn't sure you'd show — after last weekend — and not returning my calls. And now you've appeared. Like I conjured you."

"Your powers are that strong?" Janine asks.

"My love is that strong."

Janine feels the truth of that statement fill her.

Later, as Bruce does the last buffing pass over the school floors watched by his puppy, Janine and Chantel leave the dance club. They hold hands as they stroll. They chat and laugh and fall into an embrace and find each other's mouths with their own. They slide apart, but keep one arm entwined around each other as they walk. They are, very simply, in love.

A young black guy wearing a mesh, black tank top and impossibly large pants exits the club and follows them. "You sisters complain about us brothers," he shouts at their backs, "not keeping to our own. Least we still sticking to the opposite sex!"

The women keep walking. Janine pulls Chantel closer.

"Come on, my sister! You couldn't even give a brother a dance?"

Janine drops her arm from around Chantel and falls in step behind her, putting herself between Chantel and the thug.

"Bitch," the thug yells at Chantel, "come back here!"

Janine stops and faces the thug. Chantel tries to pull her along. "Come on," she pleads, "he's just drunk."

"Sir, I suggest you return to the club," Janine says in her cop voice.

"Sir? Sir! I ain't your sir! Step off, bitch, I'm talkin' to the sister," the thug closes the distance between himself and the women.

"This sister happens to be my lover. If you can't handle it, that's your problem."

"Let's go," Chantel pleads.

"Stupid spic cunt. Was I ever talking to you?"

"That's *Officer* stupid spic cunt to you."

"Ha! Dyke cop. Figures!"

Chantel steps beside Janine. "Just go home," Chantel says to the thug, "Get yourself home!"

The thug seems to calm down, but he is actually winding all of his rage into a ball. He springs, fists flailing. Janine is taken off guard. She evades the first blow, but the thug lands two blows on Chantel before Janine takes him down and pins his arms high up behind his back. When the thug struggles, she punches him in the back of the head causing his face to strike the cement, knocking him out cold. Blood streams from his broken nose.

Janine pulls her phone out of her pocket, speed dials a number, and sets the phone on the thug's back. She pulls off the thug's belt and snugs it around his wrists. She frisks him and discovers a small revolver tucked into his boot. "Asshole," she says as she slips the revolver into the back of her pants.

Her cell phone speaks: "Fifth precinct. Dispatch."

Janine looks around for Chantel. Only now does she realize that she is lying in a heap on the sidewalk. "Oh no." Janine scrambles over to her and holds her head. Chantel's cheek is bleeding and she is unconscious.

"This is Fifth Precinct. What is—"

Janine grabs her phone off the back of the thug. "This is officer Gonzales. Request ambulance and police back up to the corner of—" she looks around frantically, "Ponce and Highland. Assailant under control, but injuries..." Janine gasps back a sob. "Hurry." She snaps the phone shut and cradles Chantel in her arms.

BUCKHEAD

There are two major hospitals in Atlanta.
One, Grady Hospital—named after Henry W. Grady, editor of the *Atlanta Constitution* newspaper who was concerned that the poor people of Atlanta have access to health care—is located on the edge of Five Points in the city's core. The other, Piedmont Hospital, is located in Buckhead near an impossibly green golf course. Grady has almost one thousand beds, Piedmont has five hundred. They've both been in the city for over one hundred years.

Some things to consider: If one of the Atlanta Braves baseball players gets sick or injured, they drive past Grady Hospital on their way from Turner Field to Piedmont Hospital. If someone at the State Capital falls ill, you can bet that they will—instead of walking or taking a cab the eight hundred yards to Grady—go north to Piedmont. Chances are, if you are in Atlanta and have a choice—that is, have insurance—you'll find yourself telling the ambulance driver to head to Peachtree Road, to the best hospital in the city, Piedmont Hospital, near the Bobby Jones Golf Course.

Janine, since she is a cop, has spent plenty of time at Grady with perps or victims of crimes. She knows that Grady struggles to stay open, that the staff is dedicated to the idea that everyone should have access to good medical care even though it doesn't happen. Janine knows the acrid and solvent smells of the place, the stains on the white coats, the wobbly wheelchairs, the sticky patches, at times, on the floors. So, Janine holds Chantel's hand and tells the ambulance driver to take them to Piedmont Hospital. Chantel is alert, her neck held snugly in a brace.

Janine supports the ideals of Grady, but she's not one to trust her lover's care to that ailing system.

Getting care even at Piedmont can take some time on a busy night, and it is almost morning by the time Janine corners a young resident, a young black woman, outside the curtain hemming Chantel's bed.

"Just for another hour, then she can go home," the resident says to Janine.

"Shouldn't you do a CAT scan to see if—"

"She was only out for a minute, right?"

"She could—"

"She's alert and responsive. Reflexes and memory are intact. Observation is the normal course of—"

"I want to—have to make sure she's okay."

"Officer," the resident says, placing a hand on Janine's arm, "she's okay."

"But—"

"I can hear you," Chantel says from behind the curtain. "What's the point of the curtain, anyway?"

The resident pulls it back, the curtain glides soundlessly in the recessed track in the ceiling. Chantel holds an ice pack to the side of her face. She pulls it away, revealing her puffy cheek and two stitches.

"Relax," Chantel says to Janine. "Go to work."

"No way. I'm taking you home. I called in already."

The resident pushes Janine inside the curtain's perimeter and says, "I'll be back in an hour with the discharge papers." She looks at Janine, "Your girlfriend's fine. Relax." She draws the curtains closed again, leaving the two women alone.

Janine clenches her jaw. She hates this, hates seeing Chantel hurt, hates herself for not protecting her. Chantel reads it all in her face and says, "Come here, baby. It's okay."

"It is definitely not okay."

"Come here."

Janine sits on the end of the bed. "Here," Chantel pats the bed, "by me."

Janine moves closer and Chantel opens her arms. Janine nestles against her and is enfolded. Chantel smiles, but, from the look on Janine's face, nothing will ever be okay again.

HAPEVILLE

Two hours later, Janine helps Chantel up the stairs of the pet store.

"I can walk myself, girl. Doc said I was fine."

"That doc was younger than the both of us, and I say you're taking the day off and staying in bed." Janine feels something pull in the back waistband of her pants. She reaches back and feels the thug's small revolver still stuck there. "Damn," she whispers.

"You okay?"

"Yeah. I'm tucking you in, then I've got to change and head downtown to write up my report."

"I'd rather open the store—"

"To bed. I'll put a sign on the door and I'll come back and open it at noon, okay?"

"Who are you trying to make feel better?"

"Both of us. Now get to bed."

A few doors away, Manny wakes and the first thing he sees is Whitey sleeping with his head on the pillow next to his. This has made Manny grin every morning since Whitey first came to live with him. It hasn't yet occurred to him that his mom bought the puppy and the food and the bowls and the dog bed (that Whitey refuses to use). Manny figures that his love for Whitey has made it all come about because his love was that strong.

He wonders about the strength of love between his mom and dad, how it was weak, broken, and he worries, by extension, about the strength of the love that his parents have for him. He wonders that since the strength of his love made Whitey appear, if he, himself, will disappear if his parents stop loving him. He tries to keep these thoughts quiet in his brain, though, and concentrates on the miracle power of the love with Whitey. He is sure that Whitey's love for him will keep him real even if his parents' love fails. He knows it is that strong.

Whitey sticks out his pink tongue and Manny giggles. The giggles shake the bed and Whitey opens his eyes and grins at Manny.

GRANT PARK

Ken arrives early that same morning with Paul's groceries, his route upset by Aunt Erma's efforts to streamline things at the store. He climbs the stairs and sets the groceries next to three small UPS boxes. He's about to knock, but, instead, presses his ear against the door. The music from inside builds and swells, like something you'd hear in a church in Italy.

"Screw Aunt Erma's schedule," Ken whispers as he sits with his back against the closed door, listening, again, with Paul. He leans his head back and closes his eyes.

At this same moment, Janine is hustling up the six flights so she can change into something more comfortable to go downtown, quickly fill out the report about the assault, then hurry back to Chantel.

When the first movement of the music ends, the door snaps open. Ken yelps and reaches out to catch himself, planting his hand through the open door squarely onto Paul's bare foot. Paul screams and throws his scrawny weight against the door, slamming it on Ken's hand.

"Dude! Yow! It's me!" Ken yelps.

Paul continues to scream while repeatedly slamming the door on Ken's hand, desperate to get the door shut again.

Janine hears the screams and sprints up the last few flights to find Ken reaching into the apartment, throwing and kicking groceries and boxes with his non-slammed appendages. From her perspective, the guy is attacking Paul.

Janine reaches to her hip for her holster, but it's not there. She reaches further back and pulls out the thug's small revolver. "Step away from the door!" she yells.

Ken yelps in pain as his hand is, once again, crushed in the door.

"Step away or I'll—"

Paul screams and slams the door again. Ken contorts and says horrible things and kicks the groceries at Janine. The next slam causes Ken to kick his legs toward Janine. She pulls the trigger.

BAM!

The gun misfires.

The barrel explodes, peeling back like an opened flower.

The gun flies out of her hands and lands among the strewn groceries.

Everything freezes as the report of the shot bounces around the narrow hallway.

Ken looks up at Janine.

Paul's face presses against the slot in the open door to look at her, too.

A gash in Janine's forehead opens, then gushes blood.

"Janine!" Paul screams.

With Paul's face wedged in the door, Ken's hand is finally free. He rises on his knees facing Janine. Paul shakes and shudders and struggles to remove the chain. He opens the door wider. Paul is frozen, though, standing there. He cannot step into the hall. "Please," he whispers. "Janine. Come inside. Please."

Ken holds his arms out to Janine. Janine looks at Ken, then at Paul. Blood flows freely down her face like a fall of water. "You opened the door, Paul. With people in the hall...you opened..."

Janine collapses into Ken's arms. Ken struggles to his feet holding her. He steps over the groceries and past Paul into the apartment. Paul looks down at the twisted revolver mixed in with the scattered groceries and broken eggs. It nearly kills him, but he steps into the hall, picks up the gun and brings it inside.

He slams the door, chains and locks it.

VIRGINIA-HIGHLANDS

Stevie's face is much cleaner from his latest bath, but he is back in his rags in the dank basement. There are footsteps above and Stevie wraps his mouse in a piece of cloth and places him gently into the potato basket. The door at the top of the stairs opens and a bundle rolls down the stairs.

"Take care of it, or you don't get fed!" Lorraine yells before latching the door shut again.

Stevie stares at the bundle. Slowly, slowly, spindly legs and arms unfold. It is a boy, a little younger than Stevie. Stevie is astounded. He swallows and finds his raspy voice. "Hey...hi. I'm Stevie."

The boy stares back at him.

"You got a name?"

The boy nods.

"You want to tell me it?"

The boy nods.

"Can you talk it?"

The boy nods again and says, "CJ"

Stevie feels around the potato tendrils and says, "Want see somethin'?"

CJ nods and Stevie pulls out the mouse and unwraps him. CJ crawls closer and looks down on the whiskery head.

"Oh," CJ says. He looks up at Stevie and smiles his mostly toothless smile. "Oh."

Stevie puts a dirty hand on CJ's shoulder and says, "See? Here ain't so bad."

GRANT PARK

B ruce naps on his couch. His puppy is curled on his large chest, asleep. The puppy has grown. His back leg keeps slipping off of Bruce's rounded chest.

I nside Janine and Paul's apartment, Ken presses a folded dishtowel to Janine's forehead. Blood soaks through. Ken's other hand is bruised and swollen. Paul stands nearby, flapping his arms like he's trying to fly away. He's making a high-pitched keening noise.

"Dude. For the fiftieth time, chill! If you want to be helpful, get another towel. This one's soaked." Ken hopes that focusing on Janine will snap Paul out of the horror that Ken is now in the apartment. Paul can't cope. He's completely freaked. "Can you call the cops? Ambulance? Anything? Hold this towel, maybe?"

Paul stops keening. "She's a cop."

Ken studies Janine. "Hold this!" he orders Paul, backing off as far as he can without lifting pressure from the gash. Paul approaches and presses on the towel without touching Ken's hand. Ken pulls away and backs toward the bathroom. "Keep firm pressure on it." He finds a stack of towels and brings them back out to Paul.

"Is she…?" Paul tries to ask.

"I think she'll be okay. Head cuts just bleed like hell," Ken tries to calm him with this. "Put a new towel on it, quick. Firm pressure." Ken picks up the phone.

"No," Paul whispers.

"An ambulance maybe?"

"No. Let's wait. She—we—let's wait," Paul manages. "She'll know what to do. She always knows what to do."

Ken grabs one of the towels back, startling Paul. In the kitchen, he puts the towel in the sink and lets the water run on it. He grabs a pack of frozen peas from the freezer and gently puts it on top of his crushed hand. He turns off the water and squeezes the excess out of the towel. He approaches Janine slowly. Paul watches him and nods to allow Ken to come closer. Paul keeps pressure on the wound as Ken sits as far away from Paul as possible while still being able to reach Janine's face. He gently begins wiping the blood from her face with the wet cloth. The opera music builds in the background lending a sanctified air to their ministrations.

HAPEVILLE

Chantel lies with her head at the foot end of the bed, near the window. There is a novel open in front of her, but she's not reading. She's looking out the window for Janine's car. She sees Rita walk to the bus stop. She's wearing jeans and a t-shirt. An apron is slung over her arm. The bus pulls up and Rita gets on, then it pulls away. Chantel watches it disappear over the hill. She looks back as Bruce parks in front of the store. He gets out with his puppy. They go to the door, but it's locked. He reads the sign that says they'll open at noon. He looks at his watch. Chantel opens the window and calls down, "Bruce!"

Bruce looks around, then up.

"Hi."

"I need more food. For Puppy. Puppy food."

"I'll be right down. Give me a minute."

Bruce squats down to play with his puppy. "Who's a good boy? Who's the best boy?" The puppy goes wild.

Chantel comes to the door wearing her robe. She watches them for a moment before unlocking it. Bruce starts to walk directly to the puppy food, but hesitates when he sees Chantel's robe. He studies her bruised, swollen and stitched face, then looks up at her still happy, springy hair.

"What happened?"

Chantel can't believe that he has the capacity to notice something outside himself. This is huge. She gathers her robe tightly around her, hugging herself because she doesn't want to scare Bruce by hugging him. "Minor assault. I'm fine."

Bruce looks at her cheek, then into her eyes. "Why?"

"What do you mean?"

"Why would anyone hurt you? You're such a nice person."

Tears spill out of Chantel's eyes.

"I was with my lover. Who is a woman. Some drunk guy got mad about that."

Bruce scrunches up his forehead. "Someone hit you for that?" Chantel nods. "That's just stupid."

Chantel laughs. "Yeah. Yeah, it is."

Bruce kind of smiles back at her and Chantel can't hold back any longer. She embraces him and cries on his big shoulder. The puppy starts to run around them, yipping, but Bruce gives him a hand signal and the puppy quiets and sits. Bruce steps back when Chantel finally releases him. "We need puppy food."

Chantel dries her eyes. "Sure. Sure." She looks at the puppy. "What have you named him?"

"Puppy. Seemed to fit him."

"What will you call him when he grows up?"

"Guess we'll shorten it to 'Pup' then."

Chantel leads them to the puppy food for Puppy.

GRANT PARK

Ken puts away the groceries which he has gathered from the hall. He picks through the eggs to retrieve the whole ones from among the crushed. He rinses them off before putting them in a bowl. He does this one-handed because his bruised hand is now inside a plastic bag full of ice cubes.

Paul still sits by Janine on the couch, pressing a towel to her head. This towel has very little blood seeping through it now. Her face is clean of all traces of blood, though there are crimson streaks on her blouse and clumps of her hair are clotted with it.

Ken, done with the groceries, faces Paul, and speaks softly. "I liked your song cycle. Did you write that while you were at Curtis?"

Paul nods.

"Who performed it?"

"The Philly Lyric recorded it for NPR," Paul says. "Long time ago. Another life, maybe."

Janine begins to wake. Ken moves toward her. Janine lifts her hand to her head. "Ouch. Shit. My..." she opens her eyes and sees Paul, then Ken. "Hey! That's the guy!"

"That's Ken," Paul says patting her shoulder. "He delivers the groceries."

"Nice to meet you. Do you shoot at everyone you meet?" Ken asks.

"I shot..." Janine touches her forehead.

"Your crappy gun exploded. You caught a piece of shrapnel." Ken smirks at her. "You're lucky you have such a thick skull."

"Yeah?" Janine smirks back.

"Yeah," Ken answers. "Bounced right off."

"Lovely." Janine struggles to sit up.

"Stay," Paul says, pushing her gently back down. "It's pretty deep. We just got the bleeding stopped."

"You'll want to get it stitched," Ken offers. "And you might be concussed."

Janine sighs. The events of last night flood back and horror washes over her face. "What time is it?"

Ken checks his watch. "Twelve-thirty. Crap. I've got to get going. Aunt Erma's gonna kill me."

Janine panics. "I've got to—got—"

Ken lays his good hand on her shoulder until she relaxes. "You've got to rest." He glances at Paul and says, "Your buddy talked me out of calling the cops or medics. No one knows you tried to kill me, so it will be our little secret, officer."

Janine closes her eyes and mutters, "Jesus Christ."

"I'll check back tomorrow?" Ken looks to Paul for permission, then back at Janine. "Paul knows where to reach me if you need me before then."

Janine cannot open her eyes.

Ken dumps his bag of ice into the sink. He pitches the bag and the carton with the crushed eggs into the garbage and pulls the full trash bag. It takes a while for him to tie it up with one useless hand. He takes the bag of trash with him to the door. After a glance at Paul and Janine, he leaves, closing the apartment door carefully behind him.

"Your new friend seems nice," Janine manages without opening her eyes.

"Yeah. Please don't shoot at him again."

"I won't."

"Promise?"

"Promise. Shit, where's the—"

Paul points to the twisted revolver on the table.

"Thanks." Janine touches her bloody hair. "You think I could take a bath?"

"Sure. Stay here. I'll get it ready."

Paul starts the water running in the tub. Janine pulls the towel off her head and studies the bloody splotch. She cries the tears of the defeated. The phone rings twice and the machine picks up.

"Hey," Chantel's voice comes out of the machine. "Where are you? I thought you were coming back? Okay. I'll try your cell."

Janine twists and pulls her cell out of her pocket. She turns it off as it begins to ring. She takes several deep breaths to calm herself. She focuses on the sound of the rushing water filling the tub. She tries to feel the calmness of this sound, to let it enter her. The apartment phone rings again and the machine picks up. It is Diane, Janine's fellow officer from the precinct. "The Captain wants your butt down here to do your paperwork on this guy. Seems he's kind of connected with someone in the Mayor's office."

Janine snatches up the phone, wincing from the pain and holds it to her aching head. "Kick him. No. She doesn't want to press charges. Me either. Thanks. Oh—I twisted something in my back when I—yeah. A couple of days. Could you tell?" Janine sighs. "Thanks." Janine hangs up and slowly rises. She's woozy and holds onto the couch. Paul comes out of the bathroom and sees her swaying, but he's there, holding her, before she can fall.

Janine starts to cry. Paul looks shocked. He's never—ever—seen her cry before.

VIRGINIA HIGHLANDS

Millie shuffles into the bank and plops a stained, white apron bundle onto the teller's counter. The teller cautiously unbundles it revealing a mass of wadded dollar bills and a pile of coins.

"In the savings," Millie mutters.

"My, Millie, we haven't seen deposits like this from you in…" The teller trails off. The chaos of the currency overwhelms her. "I can give you regulation paper sleeves to roll your coins and—"

"I ain't rolling nothing. You got some kind of machine you can toss this into like at the casinos, right?"

"We do, but it's only for—"

"Do it," Millie orders.

The teller cranes her neck around for a manager, then thinks it might be easier to just do it. She slides a deposit slip across the desk to Millie. "Fill this out, please." The teller struggles with the heavy bundle to the back. Millie stares blankly at the form. The teller returns with a much lighter apron and a print-out from the coin machine. "You had forty dollars and sixty-three cents in coins."

"Coulda told you that," Mille says under her breath.

The teller puts the bundle on the counter and begins pulling out dollar bills. Millie grabs the bundle and slides the deposit slip to the teller. "Here. You do this, I'll straighten these. I have three hundred and thirty-two dollars here."

The teller fills out the form as Millie smoothes the bills.

"Business must be good."

Millie huffs.

"Your sainted daughter was in last Friday." Millie looks blank at this. "Lorraine? I can't believe she's taken in *another* foster child. Where does she get the energy?"

This is news to Millie. That Lorraine has any foster kids at all is news to Millie.

"Well, you probably know all about them. Do you help with their home schooling?"

Millie smiles wickedly. "No, that's one hundred percent Lorraine. God love her."

GRANT PARK

Janine reclines on the couch. She wears a baggy sweat suit. Her head wound is dressed with gauze and tape. On the table near her are bottles of painkillers surrounded by crumpled tissues.

She flips through the crap on daytime television, cycling the channels, not really watching anything. Paul comes out of his bedroom. "Can I make you some lunch?"

Janine shakes her head slightly and stares at the passing channels. Paul watches the TV and says, "You're making me nauseous." Janine doesn't respond, just continues to press the button on the remote. Paul tidies up the table, gathering all of her tissues. He takes them into the kitchen and throws them out.

"Ken stopped by this morning," Paul says.

"Who?"

"Ken? The guy you tried to shoot? You were still sleeping." Janine doesn't respond. "He says 'hi.'"

"Oh."

"And Chantel called again. Twice, actually." Paul waits for a reaction—any reaction—but gets none. "She wanted to come over, but I told her…maybe to wait?"

Janine stares at the television. Paul doesn't know how to help her and he hates himself for that. He retreats into his bedroom.

Janine stops flipping channels. She straightens up and puts her feet on the ground. She leans over the coffee table, picks up the phone and dials. She puts it to her ear and in a very small voice says, "Mom?"

A t Millie's Diner, Millie walks down the counter filling coffee cups. Ken sits at the counter, reading the paper. He covers his mug with his injured hand to signal he doesn't want any more coffee, but Millie pours anyway, right on his bruised, swollen hand. Ken yelps.

"Move your hand, dummy!" Millie yells.

"Cripes, lady! The hand over the mug is the universal sign for not wanting any more freakin' coffee!"

"Really? You know the universal sign for 'I don't give a rat's ass'?" Millie gives him the finger and cackles.

Ken looks around the place at all the guys eating there. "Jesus! I didn't know there were this many masochists in Atlanta!" He smirks at Millie, "Lucky for you!"

"Yep! Lucky me!" Millie cackles with delight. "I remind them all of the mother they can't bring themselves to hate."

Ken and Millie share a laugh. "Freaky old woman," Ken says.

Millie sizes up Ken with his longish hair and worn MoveOn.org t-shirt. "Hey. You look like a liberal knucklehead. You know anything about the foster kid system?"

Ken squints. "What kind of leap of logic was that?"

"Liberal bleeding hearts always want to take more of my money to give to the underprivileged." She spits out the last word. "Like I'm so goddamn privileged! So, you know anything?"

"I worked in a group foster home for a couple of summers, so, yeah. A bit."

Millie looks him over again. Someone calls for more coffee from a back booth. "Get it yourself, pinhead!" Millie yells in that direction without taking her eyes off of Ken. "Apple or cherry?"

"What?"

"Pie."

"Oh. Cherry."

Millie slices a piece of pie and serves it to Ken. When he reaches for it, she pulls it back. "Pie. For. Information."

"Deal," Ken says. "Ask away, freaky old woman." Ken digs into the pie as Millie leans over the counter toward him.

That afternoon, after his session with Dr. Vlack, Paul works on his family's backyard. There is a huge pool with a diving board, sculpted gardens, pathways, and fountains. There is a grill and outdoor bar area. A tall, brick wall encloses the spacious backyard. The cartoon family gazes through the wall of glass at their back yard. Paul clicks the door menu and selects a set of French doors. His hand shakes as he installs them. The animated family hesitates, then opens the door to the outside. They stand on the threshold together. Paul's body shakes as he watches them. The kids run outside first and jump with glee around the pool. Paul clicks one of the men and chooses the hold hands option. The men hold hands as they step into their backyard together. Paul has been holding his breath a long time, and he exhales with a shudder.

He watches how happy his family is to be outside, to be together there in the walled off space he has created. Slowly, Paul relaxes and lets their happiness seep inside to fill him.

Janine appears in the bedroom doorway. She's holding a small suitcase. Her police uniforms are slung over her shoulder on hangers. "Paul," she says. Paul still stares at the screen. "Paul," she says louder. Paul tears his eyes away from this huge moment he is sharing with his family. "I'm going home for a while."

"Home?" Paul doesn't understand. "This is your—"

"Good bye." Janine leaves and Paul listens to the apartment door open and close. Paul panics and looks back at the computer screen. He quickly gathers his computer family and gets them inside the house. When they are all safe and the game is saved, Paul turns off the monitor. He gets into bed and pulls the covers over his head.

FIVE POINTS

Rita rings up the lunches of people going through the café line. She has her eyes mostly on the trays of food and the cash register, making sure she does everything correctly. She says, "Have a nice lunch," to the departing customer as she hands them their change, then rings up the next tray of food.

"It's you," a man's voice says. Rita looks up, over the guy's security guard uniform, and up to the face of the young guard that she met in the Japanese garden.

"And it's you, Guard Man," replies Rita as she rings up his food.

"I can't believe I let you sit out there."

"I am a cousin of Miss Amy Carter's, sir," Rita says without really thinking about it. She feels related to the Carters after learning so much about them. "So I suggest you—"

"Seriously?" the guard says. "You seriously expect me to believe that?"

"Next time you see my uncle, you ask him."

"Why would you be working in the café if you were family?"

"Why would President Mr. Jimmy Carter return to growing peanuts after he was the most powerful man in the world? Why would he continue to build his own furniture, even today? Why?" The indignation grows in Rita's voice. "Because the Carters and their relatives are a hard-working people, be it toward eradicating the guinea worm in Africa, or overseeing elections in Haiti, or ringing up ya'lls lunch. We do not shy from hard work, sir."

The security guard, completely flummoxed, hands over a ten dollar bill and walks away without gathering his change.

Rita puts the bill into the drawer and leaves his change there, too, as a donation to the Carter Center.

BUCKHEAD

Janine lies under a chenille throw on the couch at her mother's condo. Her mother mixes a blender full of margaritas in the open kitchen behind her. She wears a too-short sundress. She pours the drinks and brings one to Janine. "Here you go, honey."

She sits on the couch and gingerly touches Janine's forehead. Janine winces as she peels off the gauze to reveal a row of stitches that extend into her hair. Her mother leaves the room and returns with a handful of ointments. She sits again and gently smoothes a series of ointments and creams on the wound.

"I think we can get this to heal up just fine. Most of it is above the hairline." She reapplies the gauze and smoothes the tape. "I'll make an appointment with Dr. Gupta. Meanwhile, you can sweep your hair down a bit on that side. It will make you look," she whispers the last word, "mysterious."

Janine gulps down her drink.

Another?"

Janine nods.

Her mother takes the glass into the kitchen. "Now. Enough of this foolishness. You can't stay at a job that's going to scar your pretty face. Let's write up your resignation tonight and I'll drop it by tomorrow with those hideous uniforms."

"Okay," Janine says.

Her mother is stunned, but she knows how to keep the momentum going in her favor. "And tomorrow, you'll meet Miguel. I'll have him over for lunch on the balcony. It's supposed to be a beautiful day."

"Okay."

Her mother listens for any trace of sarcasm, but finds only flat resignation. Delighted, she picks up the phone and dials Miguel. Her face brightens. "Miguel! It's Rosa. Remember me telling you about my daughter?" Her smile widens. "Yes! Yes, the one in all the photos. Well, she's staying with me for a bit and would love to have lunch with you tomorrow. How about something intimate? Here, say, noon?" She winks at Janine. "Excellent. See you then!" She almost skips back to Janine with the drink. Janine accepts it with a little girl's grin on her face. Her mother studies her. "Let's get some nice stationary for your resignation, shall we?"

The strange grin remains on Janine's face as her mother flutters around the condo searching for the perfect stationary to finally get Janine's life back on track.

GRANT PARK

Ken stands in the hallway with Paul's groceries. He checks his watch and does the four knocks again. He waits another minute, then says, "Okay, dude. I've got to run. I'm leaving your groceries and I'll check back on Friday." He pulls out a Sharpie and writes his home phone number on the outside of the brown bag. "Call me if you need anything. Either of you. Okay?" There is no answer from inside, and no sympathy from the closed door.

Outside, Ken gets on his red delivery trike. It has flames airbrushed on the fenders. He looks up to Paul's window and sees that the shades have been drawn. Ken straps on his helmet and pedals down the street.

BUCKHEAD

Janine and Miguel sit at a table for two on the spacious balcony overlooking the swimming pool twelve stories below. Janine wears a new, short sundress, much like the one her mother usually wears. It is, in fact, her mother's. Her hair is draped mysteriously over the edge of one eye, concealing her wound. Miguel does most of the talking and Janine looks at him all doe-eyed and enthralled.

"So, enough about me! What is it that you do?" he asks.

Janine's mother, dressed more demurely today, barges onto the balcony with a chilled bottle of champagne. "Oh, Janine has recently left an important position—more champagne?—with the city. She's taking some down time right now."

"So, you have free time on your hands?"

Janine's mother fills their glasses. "Maybe you can help with that, Miguel."

"Do you like to dance?" Miguel asks.

"Janine loves—"

"I love to dance," Janine interjects. She gives her mother a dismissing look and leans toward Miguel, pushing her breasts together a bit with her arms to accentuate her cleavage. Janine's mother realizes that Janine is in control now, and leaves the bottle on the table near Miguel before going inside.

"I own this great salsa club in Little Five Points," Miguel says as he picks up the bottle and tops off their glasses.

Janine smiles a sexy smile and pushes all the memories of Chantel out of her mind. She concentrates on Miguel, the angles of his face, the hardness of his body, on his masculinity and the process of submitting herself to it.

HAPEVILLE

Chantel pours fresh cedar shavings into the bunny habitat. The bruises and swelling on her face are mostly healed now, the stitches gone. The bell on the front door rings and she turns with hope on her face. It is not Janine, but Lola, Rita, Lucy and Thomasina coming in to see the new batch of puppies.

"Hi girls," she waves at them.

"Hey Chantel," they answer as they all choose a puppy off the puppy pile.

"Hair's growing in nice, Thomasina!" Chantel chuckles. "Looks cute on you!" Chantel picks up the same bunny that was in her hands when Janine brought her the flowers. She lifts it to her face and asks, "Where is she, bunny?"

Lucy puts her puppy down and the other girls motion for her to go over to Chantel. Lucy is reluctant, until Thomasina points at her short hair, then over at Chantel. Thomasina links arms with Lucy and walks with her.

Lucy begins speaking in rapid-fire, every sentence ending with an upward lilt like a question. "So Miss Giselle is not gonna pass me 'cause o Thomasina's hair? And the old ladies complaints from the Friendship Village, too? So I was wonderin' if you need help here? I'm good with pets?"

It takes Chantel a moment to break apart the fast sentences into individual words and decodes what she has asked. "Do you have any pets at home?"

"Two cats? Three fish tanks? A dog? And a hamster?"

"Where are you buying all your pet supplies?"

"Um, well, there's a big pet store over in Decatur, but well we'd start buying everything here if I got a job."

"You bet your ass," Chantel says.

Back at the puppies, Rita says to Lola, "I think I messed up at work." Lola keeps looking at her puppy, so Rita continues. "I told a security guard that I was a cousin to the Carter family." Lola still doesn't say anything, so Rita puts down her puppy and puts her hands on her hips. "I am talkin' to you, Lola!"

Lola whispers to both the puppy and Rita, "I think I'm pregnant."

Rita's hands slip off of her hips. "Does Joseph know?"

Lola shakes her head.

"You should tell Joseph," Rita says. "He's the kind of man who'll be happy he's gonna be a daddy."

"You think so?"

"I know so, girl."

Lola kisses her puppy and replaces it in the pen. She gives Rita a big hug. "Will you stand for me at my wedding?" she whispers into Rita's ear. Rita nods.

GRANT PARK—BUCKHEAD—GRANT PARK

Bruce sits at a teacher's desk, mid-shift, eating his sandwich. The puppy sits at attention, watching Bruce eat. Bruce offers his last bite to Puppy who gently takes it from his fingers and eats it, never taking his eyes off of Bruce.

"Good sandwich, Puppy?' Bruce asks. "Maybe we can make some sandwiches and have Chantel over the house. Would you like that?" Puppy wags his tail. "Yeah, we might could do that someday, Puppy. I think that's a good idea, don't you?"

At the same time, up in Buckhead, Janine's mother sits on the couch waiting for Janine to return from her dance date with Miguel. She looks at the clock. It is one-thirty in the morning. She smiles to herself, locks the door to the condo and goes to bed.

The next day, Ken stands outside Paul's apartment door holding a bag of groceries. The groceries he left last week are still in the hall.

Ken knocks harder. "Open up, dude, I'm worried! Open up or I'll have to call the super!"

The door opens on the chain and Paul looks out the gap with one bloodshot eye from the darkened apartment.

"Dude. You had me…you okay?"

Paul manages a nod.

"Janine?"

"She doesn't live here anymore."

"Can I come in? I brought you groceries."

Paul shakes his head. "Bad…time."

"Take your food inside, okay?"

"Later."

"Dude. Is there someone I can call?"

Paul slowly closes the door. Ken rests his forehead against it. "I'll check back tomorrow." He sets the groceries down. "Paul."

Ken sorts through the old groceries, bagging up anything that may have gone bad. He leaves the fresh groceries and takes the spoiled ones with him.

BUCKHEAD

Janine lounges in the sun by the pool, her mother in the chair next to her. They both wear sexy bathing suits. They watch Miguel swim laps.

Janine keeps her eyes on Miguel and says, "He asked me to move in with him."

"Already?" her mom chirps. "That's wonderful!"

"He insists that I stay at home, take care of the condo here and his house up in the mountains, too. He wants to throw big parties there for his clients. I get to plan everything!"

"I am so happy for you."

Miguel swims to the side of the pool and crooks his finger at Janine. She swings her legs off her lounge and into high heeled shoes. She stands and slinks over to him. He crooks his finger again and she bends at the waist and gives him a big kiss. He pulls away and takes a long look at her cleavage. Janine spins on her heels and slinks back to her lounge chair. Miguel watches her ass.

Janine's mother approves this most primitive of displays. As Janine sits back down, her mother says, "Nicely done."

Janine's face is passive as she gazes at the ripples bouncing off the walls of the pool from Miguel slicing through the water.

GRANT PARK

Chantel stands at Paul's door, knocking. The groceries are still there, outside in the hall. "Janine? Paul? Anybody home?"

Ken comes up the stairs with another bag of groceries and sees the bag in the hall. "Oh no," he mutters to himself. "Hi," he says to Chantel. "You a friend of theirs?"

"Yes."

"Me, too."

"I'm Janine's...girlfriend. I'm Chantel." Chantel doesn't look too sure of anything right now. Ken shakes her hand.

"Hi. Ken. Nice to meet you. I'm the guy your girlfriend tried to shoot."

"What?"

The door opens on the chain and Paul's haggard face presses into the opening.

"Dude."

"Paul. Where's Janine? They said she quit her job!"

Paul begins to cry. Chantel slowly reaches through the opening and gingerly pushes his hair off of his forehead. "Oh, honey. Let us in. We'll help."

The door closes and Ken looks like he has no hope of it ever opening again. Chantel holds up a finger, though, and nods, telling him to wait. "He's off his meds, but I think he'll..."

They hear the chain glide in the track and Paul opens the door and leaves it ajar. Chantel steps in first, turning on the light on the desk by the door. Ken scoops up the groceries and follows her.

Ken takes the groceries to the kitchen and begins sorting them. He opens the fridge and recoils from the smell. He grabs the trash can and begins to pitch stuff out. Chantel watches him, then goes into Paul's bedroom.

Paul is curled on the bed in the fetal position. Chantel shuffles between the bed and the desk to get to the window. All of Paul's plants are dried to a hopeless brown. Chantel raises the shade a few inches and lifts the sash of the window. Fresh air and light ease into the room. Paul shivers.

"When was the last time you ate, hon?" Paul doesn't answer. Chantel calls toward the kitchen. "Ken, is it?"

"Yeah."

"Can you warm up some soup?"

"Yeah, sure."

Chantel sits on the bed. "Nice new friend you got there. You're Mr. Sociable now." Paul barely has the energy to look up at her.

Later that evening, Chantel and Ken sit in the living room sipping wine. "Why did she shoot at you?" Chantel asks.

"Thought I was trying to break into the apartment."

Chantel shakes her head. "When did this happen?"

"First Monday of the month. Thing like that kind of fixes the date in one's head."

Chantel realizes that this was the morning after she was assaulted. "Oh."

"Haven't seen her since. You're her..."

"Was...I think we're broken up. Pretty sure. By now."

"She okay?" Ken asks. Chantel shrugs. "You okay?"

"I was before Janine. I'm sure I'll be fine after Janine. I am the master at being fine. It is what I do."

Ken looks at the door to Paul's bedroom. "What about him?"

"I got him to take his meds. They should start helping sometime tomorrow or the next day. If he sleeps a good chunk of that, I think he'll start pulling out of it." Chantel looks at Ken's faded and worn t-shirt. "You and Paul...?"

"Friends."

"You...?"

"Straight."

"I hear that."

"Shouldn't we get him to the hospital?"

"From what Janine told me, hospitals always do more harm than good for him. I left a message with his doctor's answering service, so he should call back soon."

"Can you stay here tonight? He seems to do better with you," Ken asks. Chantel nods. "I'll stop by in the morning. I can stay tomorrow if he'll let me." Ken stands and takes his glass to the kitchen. He rinses it and puts it into the dishwasher.

"That's nice. We'll see."

"If you see Janine, tell her I said 'hi.'"

Chantel nods, but the look on her face says that she doesn't expect to ever see Janine again. Ken picks up the two bags of trash and heads to the door. "Night, then."

"Night."

Chantel looks over at the kitchen that Ken has cleaned until it sparkles.

HAPEVILLE

All of the beauty school students stand at the front of the classroom, except for Lucy who sits beside Chantel at the back of the room. The graduating girls all wear nice dresses, their hair-dos done up special for the day, their make-up maybe a little more 'nighttime eyes' than 'graduation eyes.' They look out at their families and friends in the rows of chairs that have replaced the long tables in the classroom. Some of their younger siblings play quietly in the corner with Manny and Whitey. Joseph sits in the front row, grinning up at Lola.

Giselle speaks about this class of girls, their triumphs, their struggles. She hands out little plaques. Each one is engraved with the girl's best skill.

Lucy whispers to Chantel, "Guess Teach don't give no plaque for 'best burning off someone's hair with a perm'!"

Chantel giggles, then says, "Can't make that mistake in the pet store." Lucy nods. "Don't you let me catch you doing any perms on the dogs. And don't even think about cutting their hair."

"Deal," Lucy says.

"And so, I present the graduating class of the Margolis Beauty School. May you always remember the lessons you mastered here, and may you all make your world a little more beautiful every day." Giselle gives each girl a rolled up diploma and a hug as they file past. When they all have finished, Giselle says, "Refreshments in the backyard." The cramped room slowly empties out the back door.

Giselle and Manny and Whitey stay behind in the room. She turns to Manny and sighs. "Hey buddy."

Manny walks to her and Whitey follows.

"How would you like to live here? Upstairs?"

"Live at the school?"

"Yeah. Upstairs."

"I've never even been upstairs. Neither has Whitey."

"Well, after the party, I'll take you two up there."

"What will happen to our little house? Will Daddy move there?"

Giselle looks down at Manny. "Do you want Daddy to move there?" Manny shakes his head. "Well, I was thinking we could sell that house and live here. I could cut some hair on the weekends, so it would be easier if we lived here instead of down the block."

"And save some money, too."

Giselle stares at him, not sure how he came up with this. "We're doing fine, Manny. I don't want you to worry about anything."

"I'm not worried. I know you'll take care of me, and Whitey will take care of me, and I'll help take care of both of you. Us three are a family."

"And Daddy?" Giselle gets on her knees so she is eye to eye with Manny.

Manny slowly shakes his head.

Giselle nods. "Okay. That's fine for now, but if you ever want to see him in the future, you just have to ask."

"I don't think I will ever in the future."

"But you have to know that you can ask."

"Okay."

"Okay. Deal." Giselle shakes hands with Manny, then Manny turns to Whitey and says, "Shake!" Whitey lifts his paw and Giselle and Manny shake with the dog. "Let's go get some refreshments before Lucy eats everything!" Giselle says, and she and Manny laugh their way out the back door to join the party.

In the backyard, Rita approaches Lola and Joseph. "Hey, you two! My boss said that if there are any last minute cancellations, like the week of? Then you two can have your wedding at the Carter Center with whatever the cancelled couple has paid for!"

"Seriously?" Lola says.

"Yeah, the wedding part. Most people have light snacks and a champagne toast. You could have the bigger reception somewheres else."

"Like the VFW?" Joseph says. "My cousin and uncles are vets. They can get it cheap, and it's not booked much."

"So we have to get a DJ ready to roll when the Carter Center has a cancellation," Lola says.

"My cousin has a cool CD set-up. He can hook it to the speakers at the VFW," Joseph says. "I'll text him later about the gig."

A smile spreads over Lola's face. "We're getting married!"

"Yeah, just as soon as there's a cancellation," Rita says. Lola and Joseph embrace and then start making out in a corner of the backyard, so Rita wanders over to Giselle.

"Hey Teach. Thanks." Rita lifts her cup of fruit punch and taps it against Giselle's.

"Congratulations." They both take a sip of juice. "When are your interviews?"

"Where?"

"At those salons. The numbers I gave you?"

"Oh, yeah, you can give those to the other girls."

"I gave the best places to you, Rita. You're the best student."

"I am pursuing another avenue of employment, Teach."

"And what is that?"

"I am working at the Carter Center, in catering right now, but I have my application in to do other things. Maybe even in the library? Where all of President Mr. Carter's papers and letters are stored."

Giselle stares at Rita. "I had no idea you were interested in government, Rita."

"Not government. Just the Carters."

"And what about doing hair?"

"Weekends. Whenever. I'll keep my highlightin' skills up for sure with my sisters and their friends. It's my fall-back skill."

Giselle grins. "You go, girl."

"Oh, I'm going, Teach. I am almost GONE."

They laugh together, and Manny and Whitey look over at the sound of Giselle's laughter.

VIRGINIA HIGHLANDS

Stevie and CJ take turns feeding potato sprout leaves to the mouse. CJ pulls back his hand.

"He bite ya?" Stevie asks.

CJ shakes his head.

"What?"

"The hairs tickle."

"Whiskes. They called whiskes."

"Whiskes tickle," CJ says, then he chews on a potato leaf.

"Don't eat 'em. They make your poop runny." Stevie hands him a beat-up apple. "Eat around the brown, 'k?" He points out a brown spot to CJ. "That brown."

CJ nods. "Brown. 'K. We get food today?" CJ asks, looking up the stairs.

"Feels like a good day," Stevie says, conjuring optimism.

CJ smiles. "Me feel it, too."

AMICALOLA

Miguel's mountain house is near the Amicalola State Park, about an hour north of Atlanta. Amicalola means 'tumbling waters' in Cherokee, a name they gave to the skinny waterfall that cascades from rock ledge to rock ledge for a descent of over seven hundred feet top to bottom. The house is Miguel's retreat from the city, a place where he likes to entertain his business partners or host high roller clients from his clubs. Or maybe several women at a time when he's between girlfriends.

"And this," Miguel says with a sweep of his hand, "this is your kitchen."

Janine looks at the huge space with three sinks, colossal refrigerator, and six-burner stove. The kitchen is bigger than the apartment she shared with Paul.

"That's a Wolf," Miguel says when Janine touches the stove, "and the fridge is a Sub-Zero, of course. Familiarize yourself with everything. You can cook, right?"

Janine looks across the long space between them.

"I'll get you some help for the larger parties, but you'll have to handle the cooking for the dinner parties. And it better be good." Miguel starts to leave the room. "I'm gonna watch the game," he tosses back over his shoulder. Janine splays her hands on the black granite countertops and feels the cold seep into her palms, then slowly up her wrists and arms and into her chest and heart.

GRANT PARK

That weekend, Millie's Diner is hopping. All the regulars are there, including Bruce in a booth with his puppy asleep at his feet. At the counter, Ken sops up the last bit of egg yolk with his toast. Millie shuffles to Ken and refills his coffee. He holds his hands up like she's robbing him.

"So," Millie says as she spills his refill, "you've joined the ranks of the masochists?"

"You make good eggs."

"I'll take that as a yes."

Ken looks at Bruce's booth. "You let dogs in here?"

"When the blind are involved, yeah."

"Guy *drove* here. I saw him pull up in that huge green car!"

"Didn't say the *guy* was blind..."

Ken studies Millie's dictatorial face. "You are one freaky woman."

"Guy's got troubles. Dog helps him. End-o-discussion."

Ken slurps his coffee and asks, "You straighten out what you wanted in the foster system?"

"Yep. All figured out."

"You're welcome."

"Hell, that slice of pie didn't eat itself!"

Ken slaps down a five dollar bill and Millie eyes it. "Seven point three percent tip. You think that's all I'm worth?"

Ken stands and tosses another buck on the counter.

"Twenty-nine point two. Now yer talkin'."

"You some kind of math savant?"

"I won't even dignify that with an answer, ya bleeding liberal."

Outside Paul's apartment, Janine fumbles with her keys. She's dressed up this morning, all flowers and pastels. She gets the key in the lock and turns. The door pulls open from the inside and Chantel stands there. Chantel gasps and pulls Janine into the apartment and embraces her. Janine stiffens.

"I've been so worried," Chantel whispers into Janine's hair. She slowly releases her, and Janine retrieves her keys and closes the door. She cannot look Chantel in the eye.

"I came to get the rest of..."

"Paul's bad."

"Just came to get…"

"Did you hear me? We may be done, but you cannot run out on that poor boy."

Janine tries to step around Chantel, but Chantel blocks her.

"You closing all these doors? Steppin' into the life Mommy wants for you?"

Janine tries to get past Chantel, but Chantel shoves her hard. Janine falls back, but catches herself and stands tall again. She walks to within inches of Chantel and fixes her with an icy stare devoid of all emotion.

"I'm done here," Janine whispers the words with violence.

"What happened to the love?" Chantel asks. "Where did you put it? It was such a beautiful thing."

Janine lifts a finger in the tight space between their faces and hisses from between her clenched teeth, "We *never* happened."

Chantel's face crumples with grief and she steps back, out of Janine's way.

Janine goes to her bedroom and emerges in a few seconds with a small bag and a couple of dresses on hangers. Janine removes the apartment key from her chain and slaps it down on the desk. She leaves without looking at Chantel again. Chantel leans into the hallway and watches Janine descend the stairs. She pushes the door closed.

Paul sits up in bed. The shade and window are fully raised. The dead plants have been cleared away. Only one is left, the monster spider plant, Bartholomew. It has been trimmed back severely and all of the babies are gone, but looks like it might survive. Paul looks bad, but better than he has in many days.

"Hey, hon. How're you feelin'?"

"Was that Janine?"

"'Cause you sure look like you're feelin' better."

"She's not coming back, is she?"

"'Fraid not. But you got me. And that Ken guy said he'd stop by today. He sure seems nice."

"He's straight."

"Straight guys can be nice. I know it's odd, but there aren't any rules against it."

Paul smiles. Just a bit.

"Honey, you aren't ready for any dating show, anyway. Friends are the nice part of life. Lovers is where it gets all..." Chantel doesn't want to go any further down this path. "Want some breakfast?"

"I'm not hungry, but I'll sit with you."

Chantel cooks some eggs and bacon and some cheesy grits at the stove while Paul sets a plate on the table and two coffee cups. His hair is still wet from the shower and he's wearing fresh pjs and a robe.

"Um, thanks for saving my plant," Paul says.

"Sorry about the others. They were done."

"Yeah. The one you saved...it's my favorite. Janine gave it to me when we were in junior high."

"Long time."

"Long time," Paul echoes. "His name is Bartholomew."

"Okay," Chantel says. "The others have names?"

"No. The others were all from Janine, too, but I only named him."

"Bartholomew. Okay, then. Hey, set a plate for you, too. I see how you're looking at this bacon. There will be no stealing of the bacon offa *my* plate." Paul pulls another plate from the cupboard and sets it on the table. There are four soft knocks on the door and Paul stiffens. "I got it," Chantel says. She opens the door and Ken steps in.

"How is he—" Ken sees Paul standing at the table. "Dude! Look at you!"

Paul grins and sets another place at the table for Ken.

That night, Millie sits behind the counter in her deserted diner, hovering over a cold cup of coffee. A car parks outside and Lorraine comes to the door of the restaurant. She pushes on the glass door, but it's locked and she bounces off the outside.

Millie cackles like she's been waiting for this payoff ever since she locked the door. She laughs her way over to unlock it.

"Very funny, Mama," Lorraine says as she smoothes her skirt front.

Millie returns to her place behind the counter.

"What. What did you call me for? I don't have all night."

Millie pulls an envelope out of her apron and points to the stool across from her with it. "For this, Lorraine, I think you have time. Sit." It's more of an order than an invitation.

She sits and Millie pours out the contents of the envelope: Polaroids of Stevie and CJ in Lorraine's basement. "How did you..." Lorraine asks.

"Hell. Used to be my house. I sure as hell still know how to get inside." She spreads the photos out with her puffy hands. "I'm surprised you only have two down there. With what they pay, I figured you'd have ten. Twelve!"

Lorraine moves the photos around and picks up one of CJ and Stevie clinging to each other. The next shot shows the mouse jumping out of Stevie's hands. Another shot shows Millie's big, white-shoed foot in the shot. The next photo shows Stevie holding the squashed mouse.

"They add them slowly to homes...hell. What are you going to do with these?"

"Well, I thought about sending you to prison, you know, liberating them abused kids and sending you away? I got a chuckle out of that. But then I thought about my money."

"You mean *my* money. The money the courts awarded to *me*. For all the years of cruelty and abuse—"

"Fuck the courts, Lorraine. There ain't nothing I done to you worth my house and all that money. So, let's call this— what's the word? Extortion. You pay me back every copper penny and I don't turn you in."

"You don't have a problem with me keeping these rats in my cellar?"

"Hell. Stack 'em like cord wood if you can! You get the pictures when I have all my money."

Lorraine stands. "I learned it from you, you know. Keeping kids in the cellar."

"Hell, honey, what goes around, comes around. Just so you know, you didn't get half of what I caught as a youngster. Not even close to half. Not a tenth."

Lorraine walks to the door.

"Lorraine?"

"Yeah?"

"Social workers like to make surprise visits sometimes."

"I have a contact with the state that gives me the schedule."

Millie watches her get into her car and drive off. "You sure are your mother's daughter," she says to the fading taillights.

A couple of days later, Chantel, Ken, and Paul sit around the table eating dinner in Paul's apartment.

"Aunt Erma's finally out of her cast, so she doesn't need me living with her anymore." Ken looks to the ceiling and says, "Free at last! Free at last!"

"Are you still going to work for her?" Chantel asks.

"Yeah. Love the route, and Aunt Erma's done with the pedaling." He looks at Paul. "Hey, she said to ask you if it's possible to get grocery orders on the computer instead of the phone? She's ready to step into the new millennium."

"Sure."

"You know how to do that?"

"Sure. We'd need to set up a web site."

"She'd pay you, dude. When you're up to it."

"I feel pretty good. Doc Vlack changed my meds a bit. The new drug makes me feel pretty..." Paul trails off trying to find the right word.

"You were always pretty," Chantel interjects.

Paul chuckles.

"Normal?" Ken offers.

"God. I hate that word," Paul says.

"Fabulous?" Ken tries.

"Well, almost!" Paul says and they laugh together. "So, where are you moving?" Paul asks.

"Not sure. Want to stay close to the store. I can still do my art in Aunt Erma's basement, but I'd like another place to crash, you know?"

"I've got a room. Rent's cheap. And we get the groceries delivered. I'm doing better. You wouldn't need to worry... you've been taking care of me, and I want you to know I'm okay now."

"It's cool."

"Well, I need a roommate. And you two are the only people I let in the door."

"Most of the time," Ken chuckles.

"So I'm offering it to you two first."

"I'm happy above my store," Chantel says.

"So, what do you say, Ken?" Paul holds his breath.

LITTLE FIVE POINTS

Little Five Points is east of Five Points, out near Decatur. It's the funky part of town, the place you'd go if you wanted a vintage issue of a classic comic book, a tongue stud, artfully slashed jeans, or a handful of pills to take you off planet Earth for awhile. It is also where Miguel's salsa club is, in a renovated warehouse. Its popularity has grown and is now frequented by the hip and wealthy.

The night is late and there is, finally, a bit of a chill in the air. The camellias are beginning to bud and will bloom by Christmas. Flowers blooming at Christmas is one of the wonders of Atlanta, far enough south to make this possible, far enough north to get a good frost or even a brief snowfall in January.

This night, Miguel has taken Janine dancing. Miguel likes to go there a couple of times a week to get free drinks, check on the place, and, like tonight, show off his girl. Tonight, he pulls Janine out of the club by her wrist. When they are outside, he whirls around and puts a finger in her face.

"Don't lie to me!" he shouts. "You were looking at him!"

"No, Miguel!"

He looks at her full of fury. "I should—" Miguel shudders with rage and Janine wilts in submission.

"Baby. I love you."

This takes the edge off his anger, but Miguel doesn't loosen his grip on her wrist.

Two cops out walking their night beat approach the couple. One of the cops is Diane, Janine's old friend from Five Points, the other is a young rookie Hispanic guy. It is the rookie who speaks up, to Miguel. "Problem here, sir?"

Miguel looks at the rookie and lifts his chin. "Just making the rules plain to my girl."

The rookie is conflicted between Miguel's authority and his new cop authority.

"You know how it is," Miguel lets go of Janine's wrist and wraps his muscular arm around the rookie's shoulder. The rookie nods like they are old buddies.

Diane steps closer and recognizes Janine. Janine mouths *no* and shakes her head at Diane. "Everything okay?" Diane whispers.

Janine nods furiously.

Miguel turns. "Of course she's okay, officer! In fact, everything is so okay that we're getting engaged!"

This is news to Janine. She steps closer to Miguel who puts his arm around her as he playfully shoves the rookie on his way. The cops walk off. Diane gives the *call me* sign to Janine when she's sure that Miguel won't see. Janine concentrates on smiling up at Miguel.

"I accept," she whispers.

"Of course you do!" Miguel whoops and gathers her up like a sack of potatoes over his big shoulder. He twirls and whoops as he spanks her.

As Janine whirls by, a mixture of relief and horror washes over her face.

HAPEVILLE

From inside the pet store, Lucy watches Giselle and Manny walk past. Giselle carries a large box, and Manny pulls a wagon with another. Whitey romps by Manny's side. Lucy waves to them through the window.

"Lucy's working with Chantel now?" Manny asks.

"Yep. The world is now safe," Giselle says.

They take the boxes into the beauty school house and up the stairs.

GRANT PARK

Chantel and Bruce sit on Bruce's old couch together. It has a new quilt fitted over it. The room is otherwise the same, though, empty except for the couch and the table. They eat sandwiches that are wrapped in waxed paper like the ones Bruce eats on his job.

Puppy, about half grown now, sits near Bruce.

At Paul's apartment, Paul stands in the living room, talking on the phone. The room is dotted with Ken's moving boxes.

"Great," he says. "Do you want me to unpack the kitchen box?"

Ken is his workshop in the basement of his aunt's home about a mile away. He presses his cell phone to his ear with his shoulder as he packs a box with his wire baskets. "Naw," he says, "I'll unpack that stuff tonight, 'k?"

"Okay. Sure, I have some stuff to do," Paul answers.

"Whatcha doin'?"

"I have a session with Dr. Vlack soon. I'm going to watch my family play in their backyard a bit before that."

Ken stops what he's doing. "Like, for inspiration?"

Paul nods. "Yeah. For inspiration. Then maybe we can," Paul takes a deep breath. "I don't know. Walk the hallway after dinner?"

Ken grins. "Seriously, dude? That's righteous!"

"Yeah. Thanks. Thanks for being so excited. I don't think I could do this without you. Well, I could, but you make it easier." His grin gets even bigger. "Dude." He laughs the freest, happiest laugh ever. "Bye."

Ken says "Bye, little dude," and hangs up.

Paul hangs up and looks like he could conquer the world in this moment. He goes into his bedroom. He boots up the computer and flicks on the camera on top of the monitor. He turns to the resurrected plant on the sill, mists it and murmurs to it while the computer comes to life. He strokes the leaves and notices the new baby plant cascading off the back of it. He lifts the window sash all the way to let the late autumn light into the room. Tentatively leaning out the window, he fills his lungs with the fresh air and sticks his head out into the breeze. He closes his eyes and lets the wind play with his hair. Contentment spreads over his face and he opens his eyes. Fear creeps into his eyes, and he withdraws back into the room.

He clicks the mouse a few times. His cartoon family exits the house into the glorious backyard. All four of them are in their swimsuits. The men sit on the lounge chairs while the kids dive off the diving board and begin to swim around in the pool. The sounds of water splashing and happy, nonsensical chatter fills the room. Paul sits on the windowsill next to his plant, arms folded, watching his family play outside. He is storing up their boldness.

Paul's smile fades and he speaks to the computer screen. "No. No! That can't happen! Just get out. Get out!"

Paul frantically clicks the mouse as he shouts at the computer screen. The two kids founder in the water. "Help them!" Paul screams at the men. Paul clicks the two men into the pool. One of the kids, the girl, goes under and stops struggling. The boy sinks, too, and the cartoon dads thrash around hopelessly in the water.

"GET THEM OUT!" Paul shouts, clicking on menus, banging the mouse on the desk. He backs away from the monitor. Paul begins to wail, more animal than human.

He backs toward the open window and sits on the sill, pushing his lone plant out the window. He whirls and leans out, desperately trying to catch it. He leans past the tipping point and tumbles after the falling plant.

There is a smashing sound followed by the dull *whomp* of Paul's body on the sidewalk. The sound of water splashing from the computer fades, and it is silent. On the screen, all four people in Paul's computer family are face down, dead, in the pool.

In the corner of the silent screen, a window appears and Dr. Vlack's face comes into frame. "Good afternoon, Paul," he says. His face grows larger, then smaller in the window. "Hello? Paul? Are you there?"

Dr. Vlack checks his watch and makes a note. "Well, hopefully this means you are walking in the hallway, yes? Or maybe even outside your building right now?" Dr. Vlack nods in the little window.

"I will give this a moment, in case you are nearby and on your way." He leans back and reads through Paul's chart. His office is a lush space, done in charcoals and grays. There is a black leather couch and leather chair on one side of the office. And on the long table in between are one, two, three wire basket sculptures that Ken created.

Dr. Vlack looks at the clock, then at the computer monitor. He studies the image there: Paul's empty chair and the curtains billowing in and out of frame. The sound of sirens in the distance comes through Dr. Vlack's computer speakers.

"So, well, Paul, I guess I will just e-mail you about future session times." Dr. Vlack clicks off the link between them.

He makes a note in Paul's chart, then closes it and looks around his calming office. He stands and stretches his back, then walks over to the couch and sits. He picks up one of the metal baskets and turns it, watching how the light plays on the metals. He replaces the basket and stretches out on the couch for a short nap until his next appointment.

VIRGINIA HIGHLANDS

Stevie holds something in both of his hands.
"I see him?" CJ asks.

"No. It were you fault he got kilt."

"He kilt?"

"Told you he was!"

"What's kilt?"

"He ain't never coming back to move or eat or tickle with his whiskes. Like when we squish the night beetles."

CJ is devastated. He begins to cry. "I sorry. I sorry, Mama."

"I ain't yer Mama."

"I sorry."

Stevie kicks CJ. "You go over in the smelly room. I don't want you by me no more."

CJ cries. Stevie kicks him again, hard enough to knock him onto all fours. CJ crawls like an animal over to the dirty stall toilet.

STONE MOUNTAIN

Chantel and Ken are the only ones standing at Paul's freshly dug grave. It is within sight of the huge whale of a rock that is Stone Mountain. The casket is in the ground already. A large camellia bush blooms nearby, its happy pink and white blossoms out of place here.

Chantel takes a handful of red clay and sprinkles it onto the casket lid. Ken takes some clay and moves as if to toss it, then violently throws it overhand, ricocheting dirt off the lid. Chantel grabs his arm and Ken breaks down. They lean into each other.

"I still don't understand. I didn't even know computer people could die," Chantel says between sobs.

"Yeah. They can."

"But, he had to know that, right? Couldn't he redo it or something?"

"It was his fault."

Chantel looks at Ken.

"He put a diving board, but he forgot to put in ladders. They got tired and…" Ken takes a breath. "Even as good as he was. It was too much."

They walk arm-in-arm away from the grave.

"Poor dude," Ken whispers.

They walk together for a few moments.

"Meet me for dinner?" she says.

"Tuesday okay? I've got an art show this weekend."

"Sure."

"Fellini's? Eight?"

Chantel looks back at the gravesite. "Thought she'd show. She must be very happy in her new life."

"Hope so."

"Yeah. Me, too." Chantel looks at the camellia blooming over the cemetery. "I hope that for her."

AMICALOLA

Janine stands in the cavernous kitchen with a note pad on the black granite counter. There is a huge diamond engagement ring on her left hand, and a perpetual, frozen grin on her face. Miguel stomps around the room giving orders. "And this time, get some good tequila, okay? Not that shit you ordered last time. These are important clients. And if you ever make that crappy bean dip again, I swear I'll—"

Janine nods wordlessly.

"And for Christ's sake, wear the red dress. You're part of the show here, honey, so get with the program." Janine nods again. "That's my girl." He smacks her ass. "I'm going to watch the game. I'll call you at half-time." He pulls her close and studies her face. "Make sure you practice that thing with your tongue before then." Janine nods. "That's my girl." Miguel leaves the kitchen.

Janine continues making notes, wanting to do the very best job.

FIVE POINTS

Three days ago, Rita got word of a cancellation at the Carter Center for a wedding on the sheltered terrace. Since the weather was going to be mild, she got her boss's approval to move the set-up to the Japanese garden. Joseph and Lola, along with their families and friends, pulled everything together in three days. The VFW hall was booked for a member meeting, so Joseph and his uncles called the veterans to tell them it had been moved up by two hours and they would need to set up chairs and tables afterward for the wedding. Lola's mother baked the cake, and her aunt did all the flowers using camellias from around the neighborhood. Joseph's cousin tested the speakers at the VFW hall and rigged them to his dual CD player. Giselle altered Lola's mother's wedding gown to fit Lola, and Joseph's dad traded landscaping services for a discount on rental suits from a place in Decatur. The aunts on both sides competed to cram the ovens at the VFW with food.

The ceremony takes place in the afternoon in the Japanese garden. The weather cooperates, mild and sunny, comfortable with a suit coat or wrap. Rita stands for Lola and Joseph's DJ cousin stands for him. Friends and family members ring the small pond and watch the ceremony across the water, the words of the priest and the vows of the couple sound amplified, but it is merely the sound waves skipping on the surface of the pond like stones that never sink.

At the point in the ceremony where Lola hands her bouquet to Rita, and Rita turns to take it from her, Rita notices a black limousine pull up in front of the Carter Library.

Inside the car, the driver turns toward the elderly couple in the back seat and says, "I'm so sorry, sir, this wedding was scheduled for the terrace. Shall I drive to the rear entrance?"

"No. That's okay. It's wunnerful to see," Jimmy Carter says from the back seat.

"Didn't they get lucky with the beautiful weatha', Jimmy?" Rosalynn asks.

"They surely did," he answers.

Rita watches the driver get out and open the back door. An older white woman unfolds from the back seat and stands by the car looking down at the wedding. Rita feels she knows her, but it is only when the elderly man walks around from the other side of the car to join her that she realizes it is President Jimmy Carter and his wife, Rosalynn. The driver quietly closes the car doors and stands next to the couple, scanning the crowd for any signs of danger from the wedding party. Rita raises a hand. Both Rosalynn and Jimmy Carter give a big wave in return. Then, as the bride and groom kiss, the Carters walk arm-in-arm into the library, trailed by the Secret Service man. Rita sees the young security guard standing near the library. He is shocked by what has transpired between Rita and the Carters. Rita chuckles and nods at the security guard. The guard nods back.

Rita's day is complete. She wasn't even sure the Carters would get the invitation in time, let alone attend the wedding, but it all happened just as she had planned. And that, she thinks—this place and the attendance of the Carters—is the best gift she could ever give her friends.

ALL OVER ATLANTA

That night, while Ken weaves a wire basket in the basement of his aunt's house, while Chantel looks up from her novel and out the window over her pet store, while Janine subjects herself to the groping of Miguel and his friends, while Paul sleeps in his grave, while Stevie and CJ huddle together for warmth, while Lola and Joseph slow dance to the DJ's tune at the VFW and Rita looks on, while Lorraine pays Millie, while Manny hugs Whitey as they sleep in their new bedroom over the beauty school, while Giselle sits, watching them sleep…this is when Bruce buffs the floors of the school.

Back and forth, back and forth. Puppy sits there, ta
wagging occasionally, as his head follows the movements o.
his master, his best friend. Back and forth, back and forth.

Special Thanks:

This work was inspired by the city of Atlanta with its roads that constantly change names, its hills and red clay, fire ants and heat, the fascinating people and neighborhoods. Although I spent only a few short years inside the Perimeter, I made many lifelong friends there.

Atlanta remains fixed in my heart.

I am constantly thankful for Spalding University's MFA program and all the wonderful people associated with it. A special thanks to my mentors, Robin Lippincott, Phil Deaver, Mary Yukari Waters, and Rachel Harper. Sena Jeter Naslund, founder and director of the program, is a goddess.

I am thankful for all the friends I made at Spalding. Vickie Weaver took time to read this work and made it better with her suggestions.

My family cheers me on and this is a great help to any writer.

Loreen Niewenhuis